NICOLE DEBELLA KESSNER

Love Lost at Sea

Love Lost At Sea

© 2022 Nicole DeBella Kessner

Paperback ISBN: 978-1-66783-061-2
eBook ISBN: 978-1-66783-062-9

CONTENTS

Acknowledgments

I WANT TO THANK GOD, FIRST AND FOREMOST, FOR GUIDING me and allowing me to experience all the good in this journey called life. I want to thank my family: Christopher DeBella; Nancy DeBella; Denise DeBella-Warden; Valerie DeBella; my husband Erick Kessner; my children Kyle, Abigail, and Isabella; and My Divine Masculine, Lion. Your love has inspired me to create beautiful things. I couldn't have imagined a love that leads to a soul transformation and dreams coming true. Thank you to my editor, Lisa, who has been ever so supportive and has worked with me over the years to help me make this dream a reality. Thank you to my soul sister Rachel for coming into my life and supporting my dreams. Lastly, I want to thank all my friends and family for all your love and support. I couldn't be more blessed!

Love,

Nicole Lynne

Prologue

I WROTE <u>LOVE LOST AT SEA</u> AT A TIME WHEN MY LIFE WAS shattered by the loss and absence of my true love. The loss hit like a storm raging in the depths of the ocean of my soul, causing a darkness to rain over my life. I felt like a maiden whose true love was lost at sea … an unwitting character in a passionate love story that was painfully beautiful.

Heartache hits us all at some point in the thoroughfares of life, and when we discover that for ourselves, it is not pretty or romantic. It is torment, heaviness, and sheer agony. The loss of love can leave a person with an overwhelming sense of raw heartbreak and abandonment, hitting you in such a way that only someone who has grieved a loss of a child could truly understand.

The only imagery I could fathom in the midst of my true love's absence was of a maiden holding a lantern on the shoreline, waiting for her lover's return. She prays for his return as she sends off love letters in bottles, one by one, into the rough tides of a vast sea. She casts the letters into the churning waves, hoping that someday, somehow, her true love shall find them floating in the abyss of the dark waters, revealed by the night sky lit by a full moon and bright stars. She dreams that a glimmer of moonlight will shine upon the glass and catch his eye, allowing the bottles to carry the beautiful words of her longing and heartbreak to her lover—letters of love so true they would give him the strength to turn his compass back in her direction.

Giuseppe always loved the mystery of the sea and the smell of the salty water. She allowed him to follow his adventures and vowed to love him freely without condition.

I pray that you find your way back home. My heart is heavy in the wake of your absence. Follow the stars, my love, for they shall lead you back to me.

Love,

Serafina

Dedicated to My Forever Valentine

CHAPTER 1

~ *Finding Love* ~

IT WAS AUGUST, ALWAYS A BUSY MONTH IN THE SMALL FISH-
ing town of Midori, Italy. Since the Amalfi coast lined the town, Midori
always had some of the freshest fish in Italy. The outdoor markets sold
fresh fish and bread to the patrons crowding the small cobblestone streets
daily. The salty ocean air was alive with the smells of summer. Taffy, gelato,
and cotton candy left a sweetness in the air, along with the faint scent of
lemons characteristic throughout the region. The docks were loaded with
fishermen hard at work from dawn to dusk, bringing in the latest catches
from the nets the ships and boats brought in. Young gentlemen on bicycles
adorned with baskets of fresh cut flowers traveled the cobblestone paths.

Rocco Verratti's shop stood above the docks. Rocco was an artist
known throughout the region for the beautiful wood carvings he created
and sold to the elite tourists visiting the tiny coastal town.

Rocco's daughter, Serafina, stood in the doorway of her father's wood-working shop. Serafina was a dreamer and hopeless romantic at heart, as many seventeen-year-old girls often are. She was a beautiful young girl, native to the town of Midori. Her eyes were such an alluring shade of green that they looked as if the most exquisite emeralds had been plucked from the mines and placed into her beautifully heart-shaped, porcelain-like face. Her hair was short, dark brown in color, and cut into an angled bob that fell softly across her chin. As Serafina stood captivated by the activity on the docks below, the wind blew strands of her hair into the pink stickiness of her cherry lip gloss that glistened slightly in the sunlight.

The other girls in Serafina's family didn't share her romantic dreams. Serafina's mother, Colette, was a primary school teacher on the coast. Because of her background as well as her vocation, she was very practical.

Serafina had a younger sister, Celeste. Celeste was very different from Serafina. She was more of a realist. She didn't believe in walking around with her head in the clouds, dreaming of love. She aspired to become a teacher like their mother.

Colette kept hinting to Serafina that she was getting older and should think about following in her footsteps as well, but Serafina knew she was destined for more. She dreamed of finding her one true love—innocent and pure.

Serafina's family always told her that her heart was too big, and she was too kind and naive. They told her girls who dream of love and silly notions like romance end up hurting the most and getting their hearts broken. Still, she went on being a dreamer, despite what the others thought.

Serafina spent most of her days roaming around the village, enjoying the people and the sights. She loved Midori. The town, its people, and the coast were part of her soul.

One of Serafina's favorite places to visit was a small bookstore on the corner of Via del Gelso (Italian for Mulberry Street), a street that ran along the coastline in Midori. Whenever time allowed, Serafina would carefully walk down the small, rough, cobblestone walkways to Via del Gelso, where she was often spotted humming a sweet tune all the way to the doors of the quaint bookstore. During her visits to the bookstore, Serafina spent hours sitting at a small, rustic wooden table by a window, reading tales of love and writing in her journal while she watched the ships and fishing boats sailing in from sea at the docks below. As she watched the boats docking in the harbor, Serafina would lean her head against the glass and imagine her love sailing in to greet her upon his return from the sea.

After spending her days enjoying the town, Serafina would return to her father's shop to help him out in the evenings. She enjoyed working with her father, and the dinnertime hours usually drew heavier crowds, so her extra hands around the shop were a great help to him.

* * *

Late one evening, Rocco was getting ready to cash out the register for the day. The shop door stood open as it did most evenings when the weather was warm. Like most businesses in Midori, the shop had no air conditioning, and Rocco relied solely on two ceiling fans and the evening breeze coming in off the coast to keep the shop cool.

"Father, do you need me to lock up for you?" Serafina yelled to him from the top of the staircase that led to their small apartment above the shop.

"If you don't mind, my love," Rocco replied.

Serafina slipped on her sandals and briskly walked down the spiral staircase to the front door of the small shop. As she locked the door, she saw her father through the glass window, counting the change in the drawer of the register. She tapped on the glass, catching his attention as she made a funny face at him. He laughed and returned a silly gesture. She laughed as the lock on the door clicked loudly, then turned and rested her back on the glass door, looking up at the stars in the night sky as she silently asked God to please send her a love that was pure, true, and real.

* * *

The next morning brought a beautiful day in Midori. It was early, but Colette and Celeste were already headed down to the schoolhouse in town. Celeste always enjoyed helping their mother set up her new classroom for the start of the upcoming school year. It was August and that time was fast approaching.

Rocco had already made his way downstairs to the shop. He had some custom orders that he needed to have ready that afternoon.

Serafina was also up early, humming her favorite sweet tune as she poured herself a cup of chai tea. As she sipped her favorite morning beverage, she inhaled the spicy chai fragrance and gazed out the window at the picturesque view Midori was known for. The weather was a warm eighty-five degrees and the sky a brilliant blue, adorning a few scattered, white, fluffy clouds hanging perfectly in midair. She sighed as she took in the beautiful vista. She loved everything about this town … if only she could find true love.

Serafina gulped down her chai and headed off up the stairs to get dressed. She opened her wardrobe full of mostly sundresses to choose an outfit for the day. Serafina had an extraordinary obsession with sundresses and had more of them than most girls in Midori, and sandals were her favorite footwear during those hot summer months.

The clock on the kitchen wall played a musical medley at the top of the hour. Nine o'clock in the morning had come quickly. The little bookstore would open in a matter of minutes, Serafina thought to herself excitedly. She quickly pulled her sunflower sundress over her head and slipped on her sandals, then put on a bit of blush and eyeliner. She had beautiful, long dark lashes that needed no mascara. She took one last peek in the mirror, twirling around in her sundress before heading out the door.

The walk down the cobblestone path was starting to crowd up as street vendors slowly trickled in, setting up their stands for the new day ahead. Serafina waved at those she knew, greeting them with a smile and a kind, "Good morning." She carried on, humming a soft love song serenade as she dreamily drifted towards the coastline. *One day I shall find my love ... my forever, my heart and soul,* she dreamed as she swished her pretty sundress. She lifted her chin to the clouds that were perfectly placed in the sky like white posh pillows on the lightest blue of an antique sofa. Suddenly, the sound of the bells on the bookstore door caught her attention, and she picked up her pace, swiftly heading off in their direction.

"Serafina!" Vincenzo, the store owner, called out. "Looking beautiful today," he said in his broken English.

Serafina smiled and thanked him for her chair he had waiting for her. He knew she liked the seat closest to the window, overlooking the coast.

"Your English is getting so much stronger, Vincenzo. Mother said she has been teaching you in the evenings again," Serafina said lovingly. She knew that Vincenzo really wanted to learn to speak English fluently, and whenever he got a chance, he practiced with her and anyone else who spoke English. His dream had been to become a teacher and move to the United States where he would teach Italian, but because his parents got ill, and he had to take care of them, he never had the opportunity to finish his college degree. Books were his second love, and he did adore his hometown of Midori, so he was content with his little bookshop.

"Your mother is very kind, very loved, and a good woman, Serafina," he complimented. They exchanged pleasantries quickly as she took her seat in the wooden chair and took out her notebook.

Serafina's mother was from the United States. She taught English to her students in Midori and sometimes tutored others, including Vincenzo, who had an interest in learning her native language. She enjoyed helping people and liked the opportunity to earn a little extra money.

A native of Midori, Serafina's father spoke Italian fluently; however, he also spoke English. Colette's Italian was steady and fluent, but she preferred to speak her native language at home. Because Rocco adored her, he happily obliged, and the family spoke primarily English at home.

When Rocco turned seventeen, he decided to leave Midori and head to the United States to "find himself." Soon after he arrived in the United States, he met Colette, and his intention changed. Although she was only sixteen at the time, within a few months they fell in love, got married, and moved back to Italy together.

It was an easy decision for Colette to leave the United States with her new husband, one she never regretted. She had lived a very difficult life and had no real family. Her father had abandoned her at a very young age, leaving her with her mother who lived a life of sin on the streets of Las Vegas and considered her daughter a hindrance. From the moment she and Rocco met, Colette felt cherished for the first time in her life. She was happy to move to Midori with her new love, and she always called him her superhero because as far as she was concerned, he saved her life.

One day I shall find a love like that, Serafina thought to herself as she looked out the window at the boats pulling into the docks. She grabbed her pen from her satchel and began writing poems in her notebook—sugary sweet poems of love and romance, as usual. She poured out her heart's desires in the blank pages within the soft, brown, Italian leather binding. She dreamed of a fair-haired man who flaunted baby-blue eyes and a muscular frame, a man who was sweet, loving, and incredibly kind.

Vincenzo returned to Serafina's table with a small yellow teacup adorned with pink roses. "I brought you some tea, dear Serafina," he said warmly, placing the cup in front of her.

"Thank you so much," she smiled sweetly back at him. He departed as quickly as he arrived, and Serafina slowly sipped her tea as she picked up her pen and continued to write.

* * *

Oh my, look at the time! Serafina thought as she looked up at the large clock on the bookstore wall. It was already mid-afternoon and she needed to get back to the shop to help her father. She quickly closed her notebook and put it away in her satchel.

"Leaving already?" Vincenzo questioned from the desk.

"Yes, Father is expecting me," Serafina replied kindly. She walked over and paid him for her tea before hurrying out the door.

As Serafina walked briskly up the old, familiar, cobblestone path, she suddenly heard a whistle, and it stopped her in her tracks. She looked around but saw nothing unusual, so she continued walking towards the shop, making it only a few feet further before she heard the whistle again. This time it was followed by laughter. She looked all around, feeling confused and a little uneasy while she kept walking, as she heard yet another whistle and more laughter.

Serafina looked up to her left where the docks were. There stood two young fishermen on the dock. Fishermen in Midori were always known to be troublemakers … lowlifes and riffraff … so Serafina put her guard up further.

"Hey, honey," one dark-haired fisherman called out. Looking appalled, Serafina blew him off as she continued walking a bit quicker than before. She felt herself blushing as she held her head down and clutched her satchel.

Suddenly fear hit her like a brick wall. Feeling vulnerable, she broke into a run but stumbled, and as she reached out to right herself, she dropped her bag, sending all her belongings spilling out across the cobblestone path. She dropped to her hands and knees, hurriedly grabbing her things and shoving them back into her bag, when another pair of hands appeared in view, snatching her bag from off the walkway and out of her hands.

Her heart racing in fear, Serafina looked up to see if the hands belonged to a helper or a predator and found herself gazing into the beautiful blue eyes of a handsome stranger. He had dirty blond hair, and his facial scruff suggested he hadn't shaved in a couple days. She froze for a moment as she took in the fisherman's appearance. Those lovely blue eyes met Serafina's as he grabbed her under the arm, helping her back up onto her feet with hands that were dirty and rough but also gentle.

"I'm really sorry about my friend," the blue-eyed fisherman said in a deep, husky voice. Speechless, Serafina just looked at him in a mixture of surprise and awe.

"Oh, I mean—," he said as he pulled out a small English-to-Italian dictionary from his dirty pants pocket.

"No, it's okay. I speak English," she said softly, continuing to gaze into his beautiful eyes.

"My name is Giuseppe," he said. "Joseph, in English," he laughed.

Serafina's fear was receding, but now her heart fluttered nervously. She found herself a bit breathless in his presence as she lost herself in his deep blue eyes and his deep voice that was surprisingly calming.

"I wonder, how does a Giuseppe get away with knowing such little Italian?" Serafina laughed in return.

"I am from the United States," he said. "My grandparents live here in Midori."

"My name is Serafina," she said coyly, biting her bottom lip.

"It is a pleasure to meet you, Serafina. Maybe we will see each other again sometime soon," he said as he gently handed her satchel back over to her.

She took her bag back and watched as Giuseppe slowly walked back towards the wooden staircase leading up to the dock. She stood there watching him until he reached the staircase and turned back to look at her. He gave her a smile and a small wave goodbye as he climbed the stairs. Serafina had to catch her breath for a moment, then collected herself and began to walk towards her father's shop once again.

CHAPTER 2

~ We Shall Meet Again ~

ROCCO WAS WORKING IN THE BACK OF THE SHOP WHEN Serafina arrived.

"How was your day, sweetheart?" he asked, looking up as he heard the door opening.

Serafina was silent. She just ambled around the shop, lost in her thoughts of the blue eyes that pierced her soul just short of thirty minutes ago.

"Serafina? How was your day?" Rocco asked again when she didn't answer him.

"It was good," she mumbled back, sounding like she was in a daze. He just looked over at her and shook his head. He figured she was lost in one of her silly daydreams again.

The shop started filling up quickly soon after Serafina arrived. She loved interacting with the customers and playing with the children that came in, so she moved her encounter with the handsome fisherman to the back of her mind as she engaged with the shop visitors.

* * *

It had been a long, tiresome evening. When closing time arrived, Serafina could tell her father was exhausted from carving wood and minding the shop all day, so she told him she would close out the register and lock up for the night. Rocco readily accepted her offer and kissed her on the forehead as he stretched out his arms towards the ceiling, letting out a yawn.

"Goodnight, Father. I'll be upstairs after I lock up," she said to him with a smile. She gently touched his shoulder and pointed him in the direction of the stairway leading to their apartment.

After her father went upstairs to rest, Serafina stood at the small cash register counting the money in the drawer containing the day's earnings. Her mother would take the bag of their profits to the bank in the morning.

After counting the money, Serafina carefully placed it in the green leather pouch Rocco kept under the drawer and locked the pouch away in the small safe under the counter. She grabbed the keys off the till and headed to the glass door in front of the store, hesitating a moment before stepping outside.

The evening air outside was warm and breezy. The darkness revealed the luminescence of even very small twinkling stars, and the scent of saltwater lingered in the air. Serafina looked up, taking it all in as she drew a deep breath and pressed her back to the glass door. As she closed her eyes and let out her breath, much to her surprise, those blue eyes she encountered only a few hours earlier immediately appeared in her mind … blue eyes that seemed to pierce her to her very core. She could almost feel the gentle touch of Giuseppe's work-roughened hand, and his deep, husky voice echoed in her mind. Serafina placed her hand over her heart and sighed as she smiled. She opened her eyes and looked off into the night once again before going back into the shop. She locked the door behind her and headed up the stairs, still lost in her daydreams, even in the darkness.

* * *

Morning came faster than Serafina could have imagined. She was still dozing when she heard a knock at her bedroom door. She sat up in bed and brushed the hair from her face while letting out a sleepy yawn, then lifted her arms above her head in a huge stretch, greeting the new day ahead.

"Serafina?" Colette called out through the door. "I left some pancakes out for you. Celeste and I are heading out early to the bank."

"Okay, Mother. Thank you," Serafina replied. "I am going to the bookstore this morning before I go and work with Father."

"I love you, sweetheart," her mother said softly. Then Serafina heard her footsteps fade away as she hurried down the hall.

Serafina got out of bed and fumbled through the array of sundresses adorning the racks in her closet before carefully grabbing one of her favorites off the hanger. It was a pretty, white, A-line sundress with purple flowers that Colette had bought her on her sixteenth birthday. She loved that dress. It was not only a special gift from her mother, but it held memories of a very special day for her.

Serafina's parents had thrown her a garden party. Her family and friends were all there, and there was dancing, food, and celebrating galore.

It was such a lovely day for her. She hugged the dress close to her as she reminisced.

Serafina placed the dress on her bed and quickly headed towards the bathroom to shower. She reached into the shower, turning on the hot water, and steam filled the small room as she undressed.

The hot shower water felt amazing and yet refreshing all at once as she gently washed her hair with her favorite sunflower shampoo and conditioner. Relaxed and revitalized, Serafina pulled back the shower curtain. The cold air hit her, sending shivers down her drenched skin. She quickly grabbed the fluffy white towel off the wall rack next to the shower. The warmth enveloped her as she wrapped herself in the towel and hurried back into her tiny bedroom.

She grabbed underwear and a bra from her top drawer and slipped them on before pulling the sundress over her head. Her hair was still wet as she sat on her bed, grabbing a brush off her nightstand, and brushing through the strands of her wet hair.

Serafina located her sandals just underneath her bed where she had kicked them off the night before. She slid them on her feet and stood up, grabbing her satchel off the nightstand on her way out of her bedroom.

The pancakes Colette left were delicious as always, and the fresh fruit was super sweet. In addition to Serafina's love for romance, her love for food definitely came in as a close second, especially her mother's pancakes and homemade syrup, paired with a cup of chai.

By the time Serafina finished breakfast it was nearly 10:00 a.m. She cleaned off her spot at the table and placed her dishes in the kitchen sink. She took the last sip of her chai, grabbed her satchel, and pulled out her keys as she headed out the apartment door, locking it behind her.

The air was slightly thick with humidity, with barely a trace of the breeze from the night before. The sun was out, and the sky was a clear blue as Serafina started down the cobblestone path toward the bookstore once again, but this time she stopped at the spot where she had run into Giuseppe the previous day. Her thoughts traveled back to their encounter, and she looked up at the empty dock, recalling the look of him standing there. His eyes, his touch, and his hands plagued her memories. *Where is he?* she thought to herself. She shook it off and continued walking towards the corner.

As Serafina drew closer and heard the old familiar bells chiming against the bookstore door, her thoughts of Giuseppe continued to pursue her. *It was one look and a few words,* she thought to herself. *Instead of fading, why does my memory of those brief moments with him seem to be only getting stronger?* She reached the bookstore and rushed through the door, eager to distract herself.

"Serafina!" Vincenzo shouted at the sight of her. "I will go get you some tea," he said once again in his broken English.

Serafina looked at the small wooden table and headed over to take her seat. She pulled her notebook from her satchel and started to sketch an image of Giuseppe. Along with her passion for romance and food, Serafina also had a love for the arts. She was enthralled with writing, reading, painting, sketching, music, and dancing. When she attended high school, she took as many art classes as she could squeeze into her schedule, including drawing. She was a pretty good sketch artist, to say the least.

"Your tea, bella," Vincenzo said in a soft voice as he set the yellow teacup on the table next to her.

"Thank you, kind sir," she said back, smiling warmly.

"Whatcha working on?" he asked, nodding toward the sketch in her notebook.

"A portrait of a man I met in the street yesterday," she replied with an almost dreamy look in her eyes.

"A man?" he questioned, raising on eyebrow, curiously.

"Yes, it was strange ... actually," she replied. "I was walking to Father's, and I heard a whistle. I looked up to see two men. They startled me, and I tried to hurry off, but I tripped and my satchel fell, spilling all my things. I hurried to put them back in my bag, and that is when he appeared," she explained.

"His eyes," she said as she looked back at the sketch she had drawn of Giuseppe. She grabbed her box of colored pencils and selected the dark blue pencil. Then she started coloring his eyes into his rugged face.

"Aha, so Serafina is in love," Vincenzo said happily, his eyes twinkling.

"Love?" she questioned. "What is love? I have never been in love. The only things I know about love are from stories, music, and art. People say that kind of love only exists in fairytales ... that love stories are just myths," she said as she looked through the window at the ocean, hoping with all her being that those people were wrong.

"Ah, my dear Serafina," Vincenzo said as he pulled up a chair next to her. "Let me tell you something about love," he said as he looked into her lovely green eyes filled with a combination of doubt and hope.

"In my younger days, I was a scrapper. I ran with a wild crowd. Every day, I seized the day, and never did I believe that such a foolish thing as love could exist. I lived that life for thirty-five years. It wasn't until Maria came into my life that I learned true love is real. My Maria was an angel. From the moment we met, I couldn't take my eyes off her. Her beauty radiated an unimaginable light in my eyes.

"The kidney disease slowly robbed Maria of her vitality, but up until the day I lost her, to me she was still as beautiful as the day we met. We only had five short years together before I laid her sweet soul to rest," Vincenzo said with tears in his eyes.

Serafina placed her hand on top of his, and they both sat there quietly for a few moments. Then Vincenzo stood up and placed his hand on Serafina's shoulder.

"Never give up believing, sweet Serafina," he said. Then he turned and walked off toward the back of the bookstore.

Serafina sat there just staring at the half-drawn portrait in front of her. Her gaze moved to the ocean, and she watched the waves as she contemplated everything that had transpired in the last day. Several minutes later, she picked up her pencils and continued to draw and shade the face of the man who came to her rescue the day before.

Time always went by fast at the bookstore, and before she knew it, it was time to leave again. Serafina closed her notebook and put away her pencils, then stood up to stretch out from sitting so long. She quickly grabbed her satchel, paid for her tea, and headed out the door. She glided up the cobblestone path, stopping once again at the spot where she met Giuseppe just yesterday, but when she looked up, all she saw was the empty dock.

Why did my heart ache just a bit in that moment? she wondered. He was but a mere stranger—a stranger who she shared a glance with that somehow sparked a familiarity, yet the space between them that moment they met was so calm and serene. She just couldn't shake the feeling. *Will I ever see him again?* She thought to herself. Her curiosity was getting the best of her.

Before she knew it, Serafina found herself at the bottom of the wooden staircase leading up to the dock. As she climbed the stairs, the noise from the busy dock above reached her ears. She heard the laughter and shouts of fishermen, hard at work bringing in and processing the day's catches. When she reached the top of the steps, a flurry of activity and chaos appeared before her on the busy dock, which was typical, as fishing boats arrived and departed throughout each day.

She eagerly looked around to see if she could catch a glimpse of Giuseppe, but to no avail; he wasn't there.

She sighed and turned to sit down on the top of the wooden staircase. As she did so, she saw the portrait paper sticking out of her satchel, and she grabbed it, gazing at it once again. She let out another sigh and placed it back into her bag as she grabbed the wooden railing and pulled herself up. Then she slowly climbed down the staircase and continued on her way up the cobblestone path towards her father's shop.

CHAPTER 3

~Soulful Kisses and Stolen Glances~

IT WAS CROWDED IN THE SHOP ONCE AGAIN. TIRESOME AS these recent days were, profits were always good this time of year. It really helped out for when business was slow during the off season, due to lower tourism rates.

September was just around the bend, and then Colette would start teaching again. Celeste would be starting her senior year in high school, and Serafina was to begin helping put together floral arrangements with Miss Antoinette.

Miss Antoinette owned Antoinette's Arrangements, a small, but very popular flower shop in town. All the locals depended on her for their special occasions and holidays.

Miss Antoinette was around fifty-five years old. She was tall and slender with short gray hair. Although she was attractive, she had never married, and she lived the stereotypical life of a spinster. She had somewhere around ten cats and a ton of plants.

The gossips of the town all talked about how strange Miss Antoinette was, but Serafina had always taken a liking to her. There was no doubt about it that she marched to the rhythm of her own drum, but somehow Serafina found beauty in that.

The evening at Rocco's shop was chaotic. Between being short on supply and losing an order, Serafina could not wait to kick her sandals off and climb into bed after the shop closed.

As her father was cleaning up his tools in the workshop, Serafina walked up to the glass front door of the shop to lock it for the night. She looked down as she placed her hand on the lock, gently pulling it up into the locked position. Slowly she picked her head up and as she did, she noticed a glare in the glass of the door.

She quickly unlocked the door and stepped outside. The lights were on at the dock, but the men had surely all gone home by seven, she thought to herself. She was watching through the bookstore window earlier when they all left as the last boat headed back out to sea. Seeing the lights at the dock still on, her curiosity got the best of her.

"I'll be right back, Father," Serafina yelled out as she poked her head in the shop door. "I'm going to run over to Miss Antoinette's before she closes, to ask her when she'll be needing me."

Serafina looked over across the way at the flower shop with the light still on. It wouldn't be a lie if it were true, she thought sneakily. She unlocked the door and ran across to Miss Antoinette's shop.

"Miss Antoinette?" Serafina called out as she entered the small store. "Are you here?"

"Yes, dear. Back here." Miss Antoinette answered from the small room in the back of the store. Serafina headed back towards the voice.

"Hi, Serafina!" Miss Antoinette chirped, obviously happy to see her.

"Hi," Serafina replied. "I was just coming by to see what days you will be needing me to help out here in the flower shop." Serafina continued in a questioning voice.

"Oh, dear. Okay. I haven't really come up with a schedule quite yet," said Miss Antoinette. "Can you work daily?" she questioned.

"I suppose I could during the slower months at Father's shop," Serafina replied.

"Oh, perfect," Miss Antoinette said cheerfully as she was cutting fresh flowers and making them into what looked to be some sort of wedding centerpiece.

"Those are beautiful arrangements," Serafina said, looking at the other arrangements on the counter nearby.

"Aren't they?" Miss Antoinette said, gently lifting the ivy strand adorned with beautiful white and pink baby roses. "These are for a wedding at the Waldorf," Miss Antoinette said, admiring their beauty.

The Waldorf was a beautiful setting for a wedding. It was very high-end and had an amazing view of the water from the ballroom windows upstairs. It was truly breathtaking. Serafina had only been there once when they delivered a custom table the Waldorf had ordered from her father. She was so enamored with The Waldorf that she went wandering around admiring its elegance while her father completed the transaction with the owners.

"Lovely," Serafina said as she smiled sweetly, genuinely admiring the elegant flower arrangement.

"Can you start tomorrow?" Miss Antoinette asked.

"Tomorrow?" she repeated in surprise. She didn't expect Miss Antoinette to ask her to begin so soon. "I can only work mornings until September. Then I am all yours," Serafina said with a smile.

"Perfect, I will see you tomorrow then, say … 10:00 a.m.?" Miss Antoinette asked.

"Tomorrow it is!" said Serafina, enthusiastically. "Well, I better get going since it's getting late," she said as she looked up at the clock on the wall. It was coming up on 9:00 p.m.

"Okay, dear. I will see you tomorrow, bright and early," Miss Antoinette said cheerfully.

Serafina hurried out the door of the flower shop and onto the cobblestone walkway. She looked over at the dock to see the light still shining from the fishery on top of the dock's upper deck and quickly took off towards the wooden staircase. She kicked off her sandals and held them in her hands as she ran up the staircase onto the deck.

It was dark, and the pungent smell of fish hung in the air. The moon was hanging low over the water, leaving a crescent of white light on top of the tide as the crashing waves thundered against the dock. No one was in sight. Serafina walked up onto the deck, looking out into the dark vast abyss of water.

"Serafina?" she heard the newly familiar voice call out. Her eyes widened.

Is it him? she thought.

She slowly turned around, and there he was, standing alone in the doorway of the fishery. Serafina took a moment to take in everything about him.

He stood tall and muscular, a brawny six-foot-one. He had on brown waders with suspenders that covered his white t-shirt, the short sleeves emphasizing his muscular arms. His strong but gentle hands hung relaxed by his sides. His medium-length dirty blond hair and stubble of a beard and mustache accented his chiseled face. Last but not least, she studied his deep blue eyes that had caught hers when they first met. He was, for sure, a sight to behold. Serafina's heart was skipping beats and pounding loudly in her ears. She found his presence overwhelming.

"Giuseppe?" she questioned with a gulp.

He slowly started walking towards her, and her heartbeat got louder in her ears with every step he took.

"Did you come to see me?" he asked with a smile that revealed his pearly white teeth.

"Um, what?" She replied while turning a shade of crimson red. "I saw the light on," she went on to explain.

"Oh. Yeah, I came in tonight for a late boat that is coming in around 11:00 p.m.," he said.

"I just …" Serafina said, struggling for words.

"I haven't been able to stop thinking about you either," he said as he grabbed her hand from her side.

His hand felt so warm in hers. She looked into his eyes, and he pulled her in close. As he did, she could feel the heat between them … like cosmic energy that felt as if they shared the same body in that moment. His chest and his arms felt comfortable and calm.

Giuseppe looked into her green eyes and put his hand alongside her face as he gently leaned in. Serafina took a soft breath as she leaned into the warmth of the most divine kiss she had ever experienced. It was actually the only kiss she had ever experienced, but it was exactly what she always dreamed of. She could have sworn she heard angels singing throughout the heavens.

Giuseppe pulled her in even closer and continued to kiss her. When he finally pulled away, she looked at him and saw the look in his eyes—pure love, lust, and affection. He was so gentle and yet so rugged. She felt like she already knew him well.

"Stay," he said. "I want to spend time with you," he whispered in her ear.

"I can't. I have work in the morning, and it's my first day. I can't be late," she hurriedly explained.

"Well, I am sure you get a lunch break at work. Right?" he asked.

"I'm sure," she replied, smiling.

"So, what does a beautiful woman like you do, Miss Serafina?" he pried.

"I am working for Miss Antoinette," she said as she pointed down toward the little shop in town below the dock.

"Really? My grandmother knows Miss Antoinette pretty well," he said, as he smiled and winked at her.

"Serafina?" she heard a voice yell out from below.

"Oh, it's Father!" she said in a worried voice.

"Sneaking out to see me, are we, Miss Serafina?" he said as he grabbed her hand while she was turning towards the wooden staircase.

"Maybe I will see you for lunch soon," he said, as she pulled her hand away and dashed towards the stairs in a hurry.

"Serafina?" she heard her father call out once again, and Giuseppe laughed at the look of panic on her face.

"Yes, maybe," she said as she stopped at the top of the staircase and gave him a smile before running quickly down the stairs.

"I'm here, Father!" she called out.

Giuseppe watched from the deck as Serafina ran towards her father, and they disappeared into the shop. The shop lights turned out, and he smiled and shook his head.

* * *

Serafina lay in bed and couldn't stop smiling as she remembered that amazing kiss on the dock. She pressed her fingertips to her lips, recalling how soft and sweet his lips felt on hers. She drifted off to sleep almost floating on air.

It was an early 8:00 a.m. when she awoke. Morning had come too fast. She pulled herself out of bed and stumbled into the kitchen to have breakfast.

Colette was cooking French toast, and Celeste was in the shower. Rocco had already gone downstairs to work on some jobs they had gotten last night.

"So, today is your first day with Miss Antoinette?" her mother asked.

"Yes," she said, smiling as she watched her mother place a plate of French toast in front of her.

"I have orientation for my students today so I won't be home until later this evening," Colette said. "I can't wait to hear all about your first day."

Serafina didn't reply. She was slowly eating her breakfast and still daydreaming about what happened last night night on the dock.

"Is everything okay, dear?" Colette asked.

"Oh, yes, just fine," she said as she quickly ate her breakfast. She heard the shower turn off and headed over to the sink to place her dish in it.

"I am going to get ready for work," Serafina told her mother, and she headed towards the small bathroom.

* * *

It was approaching 9:30 a.m., and as usual, Serafina was rummaging through her closet looking for the perfect sundress to wear. She wanted to look nice in case Giuseppe decided to pop into work to see her.

She spotted a pretty pink sundress in the back of her closet that still had the tags on it. She took it out and quickly put it on. She doused on some soft vanilla perfume and put on a hint of makeup. Then, with one last glance at the mirror, she slid on her sandals and headed downstairs and out the door.

It was another beautiful day in Midori. The sun was shining, and the sky was a baby blue hue. Serafina stepped out onto the cobblestone path and headed towards the small flower shop. She quickly approached the door and walked in.

"Hello, Serafina," Miss Antoinette said with a smile.

"Hello," she replied.

"Are you ready to put together some arrangements?"

"Sure am!" Serafina replied cheerfully.

"Then let's get started!" Miss Antoinette said as she walked Serafina back to the small room with a large table, refrigerators containing different types of flowers, and shelves containing ribbons and colored cellophane wraps.

"This is where I do all of my art," Miss Antoinette said proudly, her eyes sparkling.

"Art. I never thought about it that way before," Seraphina said.

"Oh yes, flowers are most certainly a beautiful medium for creating art. You can decorate them and work them into designs, bouquets, and arches. It's so rewarding to begin with a flower that is already beautiful, and mold it into a magnificent piece of art … art that brings others happiness and love," Miss Antoinette explained.

"Do you remember the centerpieces I showed you last night?" Miss Antoinette asked.

"Yes," Serafina replied.

"Well, today you are going to be helping me put those together," Miss Antoinette said happily.

Suddenly, a calico kitten appeared on the table in front of them.

"Daisy, get down, baby," Miss Antoinette said as she waved the small cat off the table.

"That's Daisy. She is my youngest baby," she said. "You're ok with cats, right, Serafina?"

"Yes ma'am, I am," Serafina replied.

"Good. Daisy lives here at the shop. She keeps me good company on lonely days. I named her Daisy after my very favorite flower," Miss Antoinette said with a smile.

"Okay, Serafina, here is the ivy vine, and to your left there are the pink and white roses in the refrigerator. The ribbon is to your right on the shelves." Miss Antoinette went on giving Serafina the rundown on everything's location. She then grabbed some flowers from the fridge and continued on, showing her how to construct the beautiful centerpieces. Serafina fumbled a bit at first but soon caught the hang of it.

"Good job, Serafina. It seems you're a natural," Miss Antoinette said smiling. Serafina smiled back, pleased that she was off to a good start.

"We need to make fifty of these by the end of the week, and I am going to take you with me to the Waldorf to help set up the tables for the wedding." Miss Antoinette said.

"Really?" Serafina said with excitement in her eyes.

"Of course, dear. I can't do that job all by myself. I need your help." Miss Antoinette said encouragingly.

Serafina was happy that Miss Antoinette already seemed pleased with her work and was trusting her to help decorate for the wedding. So far, this job was going even better than Serafina had hoped.

The two of them worked together all morning on the centerpieces, except when Miss Antoinette had to disappear to the front of the store every now and then to help a customer. It gave Serafina another boost to her confidence to know that Miss Antoinette didn't feel the need to watch over her every minute, even though it was only her first day.

While they were working, Serafina saw an old radio sitting on the shelf in the corner of the room.

"Does that work?" she asked, pointing to the radio.

"I haven't used it in ages, but I am sure it does," Miss Antoinette answered. "I guess I usually find myself just enjoying the quiet while I work in the shop."

"Can I try it?" she asked.

"Sure, dear," Miss Antoinette replied.

Serafina took the old radio down off the shelf, blew the dust off of it, and plugged it in. It was all static at first, but she fumbled with the dial a bit, and a romantic instrumental tune came on.

"This sounds nice," Serafina said, and Miss Antoinette nodded in agreement. The morning flew by as the two of them listened to the music on the radio while they also worked together in harmony.

"It seems it's time for lunch already," Miss Antoinette said, looking at the clock above the door that read noon. Serafina also looked up at the clock, surprised to see the time.

"I usually bring my lunch, Serafina, but you are more than welcome to leave to get something to eat as long as you are back by 1:00 p.m.," Miss Antoinette said with a smile.

"Okay, great," Serafina said as she quickly cleaned up her work spot.

She walked out of the small shop and over to the lunch cart across the street where she ordered a slice of cheese pizza and a Diet Coke. As she stood waiting for her food, she looked up at the dock and saw the fishermen hard at work. She wondered if Giuseppe was up there.

Serafina sat down with her food on the small bench outside the flower shop and daydreamed about the kiss she and Giuseppe shared the night before. *Was he thinking of me too?* she wondered. As she enjoyed her food, her daydreams, and the charming sounds of Midori, the hour passed by quickly, and before she knew it, it was time to return to the flower shop.

"Back to work," she said to Miss Antoinette with a smile as she happily entered the shop.

It was around 3:00 p.m. when Serafina finished up for the day. "You did a great job today, Serafina. I will see you again tomorrow?" Miss Antoinette questioned.

"Yes, ma'am. I'll be here at 10:00 a.m. sharp," she replied.

Serafina's father had been busy most of the day, and he was delighted to see Serafina when she returned to his shop.

"Thank God, Serafina," he said. "Can you go check out the customers?"

"Sure, Father," she replied. There was a line of three customers already waiting to check out when she got to the register.

That night Serafina was worn out from working all day, first in the flower shop and then with her father. When Rocco saw how tired she was, he told her he would close up so she could take off a bit early.

"Thanks, Father. I will see you upstairs," she said.

Serafina walked out the door and climbed the stairs to the small apartment. She ran to her bedroom and slipped on her nightgown. She crawled into bed and was asleep before her head could even hit the pillow.

CHAPTER 4

~ A Rose Is But A Rose ~

IT WAS RAINY AND OVERCAST IN THE SMALL TOWN OF MIDORI. September was finally here, and that meant Serafina would be working full time with Miss Antoinette. It had also been about a week since she had last seen Giuseppe.

Today was the day Serafina and Miss Antoinette were going to the Waldorf to set up the tables for the wedding, and Serafina was eager to go back to the elegant hotel. She had gotten up early, quickly showered, dressed, and grabbed her umbrella before heading to the flower shop. She was really looking forward to the day.

"Hello," Miss Antoinette said cheerfully as Serafina walked through the front door of the shop.

"Hello," she said, smiling.

"Are you ready to load the truck?" Miss Antoinette asked. She was carefully taking all the centerpieces and the bouquets for the wedding from the fridge and packing them into large boxes. Serafina was pleased to see how much they had accomplished since she had started working with Miss Antoinette.

"Sure am," Serafina said as she grabbed a couple of the packed boxes from the table and headed out the back door of the shop. She loaded the boxes into the back of the white truck, then went back to the shop for another load, and then another.

"This looks to be the last one," Miss Antoinette said as she handed Serafina one more box from inside the shop before climbing into the front seat of the truck. Serafina finished loading the truck then removed the rain poncho Miss Antoinette had thankfully given her, before jumping into the passenger seat.

"Oh, Serafina. I forgot to lock up the front door. Do you mind going back in and locking it up?" Miss Antoinette asked.

Serafina hopped out of the truck and ran inside quickly, trying not to get wet from the rain. She headed towards the desk at the front of the store that served as the counter. When she reached the register, she bent down to grab the key from the bottom drawer. As she did so, she heard the shop door open.

"We are closed," she said while fumbling in the drawer, looking for the key.

"How much for this?" she heard a husky, familiar voice ask. Startled, she jerked up quickly and hit her head on the lip of the granite countertop.

"Ouch!" she said as she stood up, her head throbbing. There he was, standing in front of her holding a single red rose.

"Giuseppe," she said surprised.

"Well?" he asked.

"Five euros," she said, holding her hand on her head that was still hurting. "It's one of our more expensive rose varieties."

"Highway Robbery," he laughed as he pulled out his wallet from his back pocket. "Here you go," he said as he handed her the money. She smiled as she put the money in the register.

"I'm sorry, but we really are closed," she said. "I am headed to the Waldorf to deliver arrangements for a wedding."

"The Waldorf, huh? Fancy," he said.

"Yes, it really is," she smiled.

"Well, I better not keep you too long, then," Giuseppe said as he headed towards the door while Serafina followed him with the keys. "I wanted to buy this rose for a beautiful woman I know," he said.

She looked down in disappointment and felt her cheeks redden in embarrassment. Giuseppe put his hand on her chin and lifted it up to his face.

"Here you go," he said, handing her the rose. She looked up, meeting his deep blue eyes with hers. He slowly leaned in and placed a gentle kiss on her lips.

"I can't stop thinking of you, sweet Serafina," he said.

"I'm sorry, but I really have to go," she said, cursing the timing that demanded she end this perfect moment with Giuseppe. "Miss Antoinette is waiting on me," she said, her voice and eyes both full of regret.

"I understand," he said, giving her a warm smile as he turned and left the shop.

Serafina locked the door behind him. He pressed his hand to the glass door that was decorated with beads of water from the rain. She lifted her hand on the other side of the glass and pressed it against his. He gave her one final smile, then turned to walk down the cobblestone path, putting up his hood to keep from getting wet.

Serafina looked at her rose and lifted it to her nose, inhaling its sweet scent. Even though she worked in the flower shop every day, she never tired of the beautiful smell of the flowers, and this particular rose was one of her favorites. How could Giuseppe have known?

Back on task, Serafina returned the key to the drawer behind the desk and headed out the back door. She ran to the truck and hopped in.

"What took you so long? Is everything okay?" Miss Antoinette questioned.

Serafina pulled out her rose. "This," she said, showing Miss Antoinette the rose.

"I am confused?" she questioned. Serafina smiled softly as she smelled her rose, and suddenly Miss Antoinette's eye lit up.

"A suitor?" She asked with a smile.

Serafina shyly smiled back at her but didn't answer. Miss Antoinette grinned, then put the truck in drive and headed out the back lot of the shop.

* * *

When Serafina and Miss Antoinette pulled into the parking lot of the hotel, the valet sent them around to the back entrance of the ballroom. Miss Antoinette expertly backed the truck up to the door, and they quickly got out and started unloading the boxes from the truck into the ballroom. The needed to get the flowers inside as quickly as possible to keep them fresh and protect them from the rain.

Once inside, Serafina stopped to look around her. The room was large, with fifty round tables surrounding the large wooden dance floor. She hurried over to the huge glass windows in the front of the room that overlooked the ocean and stood there for a moment just taking in the view.

"It's gorgeous, isn't it?" Miss Antoinette said.

"My goodness … yes!" Serafina said, breathlessly. "It's even prettier than I expected. I would love to get married here someday."

"You and I both!" said Miss Antoinette, laughing as she winked at Serafina. "But for now, let's get these tables set up."

* * *

Three hours later the ballroom was decked out with beautiful flower arrangements, and the smell of fresh roses filled the air. It was a vision to behold, and Serafina felt proud that she had helped create such a beautiful atmosphere.

She daydreamed of dancing on the large dance floor with Giuseppe at their wedding. She would wear the most beautiful white wedding gown, and they would glide around the dance floor, lost in each other's eyes, dancing to her favorite love song.

"Serafina?" Miss Antoinette interrupted her daydream. "Are you ready to go?" She asked.

"Yes, I guess so. It's just so lovely, I hate to leave," Serafina said.

"Okay, have one more look around, but then we need to get back to the shop," Miss Antoinette said, heading out towards the back door. Serafina looked back at the room once last time before following her out.

* * *

The rain had picked up while they were inside the hotel, and Serafina looked out the window, craning her neck at the dock as they drove by.

"Is he up there?" Miss Antoinette questioned.

"Yes," Serafina said, smiling coyly.

"I once dated a fisherman," Miss Antoinette said.

"Really?" Serafina asked, surprised. It was hard to imagine Miss Antoinette being young and in love.

"Oh yes, he was the love of my life. It was many years ago," she hesitated before continuing. "He was involved in a boating accident and drowned in stormy seas." She said, faltering. "The loss devastated me. I tried to move on, but I just couldn't," Miss Antoinette told her.

"I know they call me a spinster, and people think I'm strange. There are rumors around Midori that I have never been loved by a man, but the truth is that I was loved very much, maybe more than anyone else, ever. Now I love my kitties, and that is good enough for me," Miss Antoinette explained.

"Fishermen lead a dangerous life. The sea takes its hostages and leaves behind many victims. Just know that being a fisherman's lover is sometimes the most beautiful thing, but it can also be utterly heartbreaking as well," Miss Antoinette warned her.

Serafina looked off towards the dock through the truck window as pearls of raindrops landed and ran down the glass. Miss Antoinette pulled the truck into the back lot of the flower shop, then got out of the truck and opened the back door of the shop. Serafina followed behind her.

"I'm going to go open up the front of the store," Miss Antoinette said.

"Okay," Serafina said as she placed her satchel down under the table in the back room. She turned on the radio and hummed to the soft tune it played. There were a couple of orders that still had to be completed for the day and she started working on them right away. She wanted to continue proving herself to Miss. Antoinette. She pondered Miss Antoinette's love story as she worked.

* * *

A couple days later Serafina was closing up the flower shop after a long, busy day. Miss Antoinette wasn't feeling well so she had gone home early, leaving Serafina to tend to the day's end. She already trusted Serafina enough to let her close up the shop.

Serafina was at the register counting the profits for the day when she heard a knock at the back door. "A delivery this late?" she wondered aloud, feeling a sense of unease. She quickly locked the cash away in the small safe behind the counter and headed towards the back door.

She looked through the peephole before opening the door. It was him—Giuseppe. *Oh, my God*, she thought. She quickly dipped into the small bathroom and fixed her hair in the mirror before she opened the door.

"Giuseppe," she said, sounding surprised.

"Is this a bad time?" he asked.

"No, come in," Serafina said as she stepped aside to allow him to enter the small back room.

"I am sorry I haven't come and visited in a couple days. Work has been crazy busy," he said as he looked into her eyes.

"Yeah, here, too," she said smiling back at him.

"You look beautiful," he said, leaning in and whispering in her ear, causing her to blush.

"I can't stop thinking about you," he said. "Your green eyes are so beautiful, and the scent of vanilla in your hair haunts me," he said as he touched her hair, gently brushing it back from her face. Serafina felt herself practically swooning at his words.

"I had to come and see you," Giuseppe said. He leaned in and gently held her face as he looked into her eyes and softly kissed her lips. "Is Miss Antoinette here?" he asked.

"No, she left early today," Serafina replied. "I was just closing up the shop."

Giuseppe ran his hands over Serafina's dress and pulled her in close to his muscular chest. She was lost in the experience of him, unable to believe he was actually here with her. She relaxed into his arms as he picked her up gently and sat her on top of the table, placing delicate kisses on her neck and ear. She quivered in nervous excitement, as this was her first time to ever be touched by a man—a man whose touch she had been longing for in her dreams.

Serafina stretched her arms towards the ceiling, feeling no hesitation as Giuseppe slowly slid her dress over her head and it fell to the floor. Feeling only anticipation, Serafina kicked off her sandals as her legs dangled off the side of the table. She felt his chest and muscular arms as he removed his shirt. He kissed her passionately as he laid her body down onto the table and slowly ran his hands over her now naked body. He let his pants drop to the floor, and the radio played a soft, romantic Italian symphony in the background as their two bodies became one, making love right there on the back table.

* * *

They lay together on the table wrapped in each other's arms. Giuseppe stroked Serafina's hair and looked into her green eyes.

"Come have lunch with me tomorrow. I want to see your beautiful face every day, Serafina," he said, stroking her soft cheek.

She smiled and whispered, "Okay," as he slowly feathered her cheek with soft kisses and continued to hold her in his strong, gentle arms.

"I have to lock up soon," she said.

"I'll be waiting for you tomorrow," he said, as Serafina got up and started getting dressed, without feeling shy about her nakedness. She grabbed her dress and slid it over her head as Giuseppe retrieved his clothes and got dressed, too. While he was putting on his jacket, Serafina walked him over to the back door.

"Tomorrow!" he said again, insistently, as he gave her a lingering kiss goodbye.

"Tomorrow," she said back, grinning as she closed the door behind him. She turned and leaned against the closed door as she sighed and held her hand over her heart. She was in love; there was no doubt about it.

CHAPTER 5

~Love & War~

LUNCHTIME COULDN'T COME SOON ENOUGH. FORTUNATELY, Miss Antoinette had a lot of orders coming in for Christmas, and Serafina was more than busy putting together arrangements, so that helped the time fly by. Before she knew it, noon rolled around, and she was headed off towards the dock.

She had spent her lunchtime there with Giuseppe every day since the first night of many they spent making love. He showed her and taught her about the boats and ships and the ins and outs of fishing. He told her all about his family back in the United States and how he wanted to take her home to meet his mother and father. They spent every free moment together, whenever possible.

Serafina introduced Giuseppe to one of her other loves ... the bookstore, and they often went there together on the weekends. Vincenzo adored Giuseppe, and Giuseppe even taught him a bit more English while they visited.

Serafina's parents and Celeste even loved Giuseppe. Sometimes he would stop by her father's workshop and help him out while Serafina was busy working at the flower shop. Serafina's mother enjoyed sharing stories about the United States with him, and she loved that he was also an American native. Her eyes always twinkled when she was talking with him, and it was obvious to everyone around them that Colette approved of this young man for her daughter.

Giuseppe had also taken Serafina to meet his grandparents. They were incredibly loving and kind to her, and she adored them.

The more time Serafina and Giuseppe spent together, the stronger their feelings grew for one another. During their time together, Giuseppe told Serafina she was the most enchanting woman he had ever known, and he knew she was his home. She was everything he had ever wanted.

He told Serafina that he wanted to marry her and make her dreams come true. He wanted to give her the wedding of her dreams at the Waldorf before starting a life together either in Midori or back at his home in the United States. He knew he would be promoted to lead fisherman soon, and then he would make enough money to get her a ring. Life was beautiful for this young couple in love.

* * *

The time flew by for Giuseppe and Serafina, and Christmas came around quickly. Giuseppe had gotten a small place of his own not too far from the dock, and he was making great strides at work. He was really working hard to become lead fisherman.

He and Serafina went out to the mainland and cut down a fresh pine. They brought it back to his place and decorated it with pretty ornaments and twinkling lights. They loved sitting on the couch, drinking hot cocoa as they cuddled to keep warm on the chilly winter nights.

* * *

The Christmas season was a flurry of activity at Miss Antoinette's, and Serafina fell into bed exhausted each night, but in January things calmed down at the flower shop. Miss Antoinette told Serafina not to get too excited about the slower pace, as the Valentine's Day rush was just around the corner.

Throughout the past few months, Serafina and Miss Antoinette had become very close. She greatly admired Miss Antoinette, who was becoming like a second mother to her.

With Valentine's Day approaching, Serafina and Giuseppe decided to set Miss Antoinette up on a date with Vincenzo. The young couple thought Vincenzo and Miss Antoinette would get along well together. Plus, they had both had lost their lovers at an early age and were essentially alone.

Miss Antoinette was unsure of the idea at first. She hadn't been out with a man in years, but Serafina talked her into giving it a try.

"It will be fun," Serafina said, continuing to convince Miss Antoinette, as she did her hair and makeup.

Vincenzo, on the other hand, couldn't wait. Giuseppe helped him pick out his best attire for the big night.

Their date was at the coffee shop on Via del Gelso. Serafina walked Miss Antoinette down to the shop as she calmed her nerves, while Giuseppe was giving Vincenzo pointers as they waited, anxiously, for Miss Antoinette to arrive.

Each time the bells on the door of the coffee shop rang, Giuseppe eagerly looked up to see who was entering. When Miss Antoinette finally walked in, accompanied by Serafina, Giuseppe let out a sigh of relief, as if it were he who had the date with Miss Antoinette. He gestured for Vincenzo to stand and handed him a single daisy to give to Miss Antoinette. Following behind Miss Antoinette, Serafina saw her hesitate and gave her a small push on the back towards Vincenzo.

"Bella," Vincenzo greeted her as he held out his hand holding the daisy. Miss Antoinette looked at the flower.

"A daisy," she said.

"They are your favorite, no?" Vincenzo asked, worried.

"Yes, they are," she admitted.

Vincenzo took Miss Antoinette by the hand and pulled out a chair for her.

"Good luck, buddy," Giuseppe said as he patted Vincenzo on the back. He walked over to Serafina and grabbed her hand. They looked over at Miss Antoinette and Vincenzo and saw the two of them already laughing and talking. Giuseppe kissed Serafina happily.

"I think it's a love connection," he said, smiling at her.

"I think so too," she said, giggling as they walked out of the small coffee shop and headed back to Giuseppe's place.

* * *

It was almost Valentine's Day and Miss Antoinette and Vincenzo had become an item for sure. No one in town had ever seen the two of them so happy.

It was incredibly busy at the flower shop, nearly making the Christmas rush seem tranquil. Orders were coming in like crazy, and some nights Serafina left the flower shop beyond tired.

Giuseppe had been busy as well. He had been working a lot of overtime on the dock, trying to save up money to buy Serafina an engagement ring and take her home to meet his parents in the United States. Their busy schedules didn't leave much time in between for them to see each other.

* * *

Finally, the day was here. Valentines Day! The shop was bustling with customers. It was nearly overflowing with fresh flowers, and their scent was almost overwhelming. Gentlemen from all over town and the nearby area swarmed the shop looking for the perfect flowers for their significant others. It seemed that the spirit of love and romance had invaded the town overnight.

Serafina and Miss Antoinette ran around the shop all day without stopping. Between pre-orders and last-minute purchases, they suggested, cut, and arranged flowers all day long, constantly trying to help their customers find the perfect arrangement for that special person. By the end of the day, the shop was nearly empty of flowers, and the back room was a wreck. Serafina was cleaning it up when Miss Antoinette came back from the front of the shop and joined her.

"We sold over thirty dozen roses today," Miss Antoinette said.

"That is great," Serafina said as she rushed around the room, continuing to clean, barely listening to Miss Antoinette.

"This is for you, Serafina," Miss Antoinette said, handing Serafina a box wrapped in pretty red paper when she stopped and looked up at her.

"What is it?" Serafina questioned, feeling awkward.

"Go ahead. Open it," Miss Antoinette urged with a smile. Serafina untangled the sheer, red bow that was wrapped around the box covered in shiny crimson red paper. She ripped the paper to reveal a white shirt box underneath. She opened the box, and the inside was lined with pink tissue paper.

"A black strapless dress!" Serafina said as she held it up to her body, adoring its beauty. A paper heart was inside the box, and it was inscribed with a message. "A little black dress for my Italian princess. –Giuseppe." She sighed happily, smiling as she read his message.

"Well go ahead; put it on. He is waiting!" Miss Antoinette said with a smile, clapping her hands.

Serafina ran to the bathroom and closed the door. Five minutes went by before she emerged from the bathroom in the sexy little black dress.

"You look stunning, my dear," Miss Antoinette said. "You just need a bit of a touch in your hair." She grabbed a baby red rose and a small hairpin off the table. She walked over to Serafina and pinned her hair back with the flower.

"There," she said. "Perfect."

"Not quite," Serafina said. She grabbed her satchel, pulled out her pink, cherry lip gloss, and applied it. "Okay, now I'm ready."

"These are from me and Vincenzo," Miss Antoinette said as she handed Serafina a box wrapped in pretty, pink paper with a white satin bow.

Serafina tore open the paper and opened the box. It contained a pair of beautiful, black leather heels and a blank envelope.

"Open it," Miss Antoinette said.

Serafina opened the envelope, and tears filled her eyes. Inside the envelope were two tickets to the Valentines' Day Ball at the Waldorf and a one-night stay at the hotel.

"Oh, my God!" she cried, looking up at Miss Antoinette, incredulous.

"Serafina, you haven't only given me the gift of a family again, but you have given me true love. I thought I could never again find happiness with a partner at my old age, but you proved me wrong. You deserve a wonderful night, sweetheart," Miss Antoinette said, hugging Serafina tightly. "Now go, Serafina. Giuseppe is waiting on you," she said as she rushed her out the back door.

* * *

When Serafina walked up to the Waldorf, Giuseppe was waiting for her at the door, holding a single pink rose. The sight of him standing in front of the large, elegant hotel took her breath away. He was dressed in a black, fine Italian suit, and he was clean shaven. *He looks utterly handsome,* she thought to herself.

The look in Giuseppe's eyes when he saw Serafina approaching set her heart on fire. He grabbed her hand as she walked closer to him.

"Amore mio. Sei la donna piú bell ache abbia mai visto," he said in her ear as he pulled her in close to him. "How is that for my Italian?" he asked.

"Magnifico. And you are the most handsome man I have ever laid eyes on, as well," she replied as she giggled.

"Let's go in, my love," he took her hand and walked her into the large lobby with its beautiful, vaulted ceilings that she loved so much. The marble floor displayed a large Waldorf "W" logo. Waiters lined the aisle holding trays of champagne with strawberry slices in them. Serafina grabbed one of the glasses off of a tray as they headed through the double doors into the ballroom.

The ballroom was large, just as Serafina remembered. The enormous chandelier hanging over the large wooden dance floor at the center of the room was comprised of hundreds of crystal facets that sparkled brilliantly even in the dimly lit room. The round tables were clothed in black tablecloths and arrayed with the finest silver and crystal. Towers of red roses spilled out of the centerpieces, with vines of green ivy hanging down their sides onto the black linen, and they were accented all around by tea candles. The lighting in the room was dim, and the large window that faced the ocean was decorated by the stars shining brightly in the deep, black, cloudless sky. The waiter led them through the elegant room to their table by the window.

"My love," Giuseppe said as he pulled out Serafina's chair. She smiled at him as she took a seat.

"Wow," she said as she stared out the window into the starlit sky. "This is beautiful. A dream come true."

"My love, since the day I met you my life has been nothing short of amazing. You make me so complete and happy. You are my heart and soul. There is not a day that goes by where I don't try to be a better man for you." He got down on one knee in front of her chair.

"Will you be my wife, Serafina?" He asked, looking into her eyes as he pulled out a small black box and opened it. Inside was a beautiful, heart-shaped diamond solitaire. Serafina's hands flew to her mouth in total surprise as tears formed in her eyes, spilling down her cheeks.

"Be my forever valentine, Serafina, not just today, but always," he said as he looked up at her.

"Yes!" she practically squealed as she cried tears of happiness. Giuseppe kissed her softly, and a tear escaped his eye.

"I have some good news I want to share with you about work, but that can wait," Giuseppe said. "This is your night, Serafina." He grabbed her hand and pulled her up out of her chair, leading her onto the dance floor and pulling her in close to him.

The band was playing a soft piano melody. They danced slowly as Serafina laid her head against Giuseppe's chest and listened to the sound of his heart. She closed her eyes, feeling totally loved and quite complete.

* * *

The night was beyond amazing. At the end of the evening, they headed up the crystal elevator in the middle of the lobby to their room.

"Door number nine," he said as they exited on their floor. "Ahh, here we are," he said as he opened the door.

The room was spacious and had a huge window overlooking the ocean and sky, just like the ballroom. The bed was big, and the comforter looked like large white pillows. There were red rose petals lining a trail to the bed, with candles lit all around the room. It was truly the perfect room for them.

Giuseppe led Serafina to the bed and slipped off her black leather heels. He kissed her lips, still softly as ever, but tonight there was a passion and urgency to his kisses. He gently planted sensuous kisses down her neck and onto her shoulders, sending shivers of passion down her spine. He kissed her across her chest and slid her dress down off her shoulders, letting it fall to the floor. He continued to run his mouth down her body to her belly button. Then he reached her panties, grabbing them with his teeth as he slid them down to the floor.

Serafina felt heat rise up to the top of her head. As she stepped out of her panties, Giuseppe picked her up and laid her onto the soft, fluffy bed, then trailed her body with kisses all the way back up to her chin.

Full of anticipation, Serafina grabbed his shirt and slowly unbuttoned it, feeling his broad shoulders and muscular arms as she peeled it off of him. She reached down and undid his zipper as she raised her feet upwards and slid his pants down off his body. He kissed her hard with passion, as they sensed one another's need. He pushed her legs apart with his legs as he slid deep inside her, and she gasped as he looked into her eyes. He continued thrusting deeply inside her wanting to be so far inside her that they would almost become one.

Serafina moaned in pleasure. She loved the feel of his large, muscular frame. It felt so good on top of her small body and his erection was so large and swollen that with every thrust it felt like he was getting bigger. They made love over and over that night, only stopping for small naps in between. It was the best night of her life.

* * *

The next morning the newly engaged couple welcomed the new day by enjoying a room service breakfast in bed. After relaxing and just enjoying the last few minutes of their overnight getaway, they knew they needed to get moving. Giuseppe had to go down to the dock to help out one of the crews. They took a quick shower together to freshen up after their night of lovemaking before getting dressed, saying farewell to their beautiful hotel room, and checking out. Serafina was glowing as they stepped onto the elevator. She couldn't stop staring at her beautiful ring.

They kissed goodbye at the end of the hotel's driveway, then Serafina rushed home to tell her mother, father, and Celeste the good news. When she showed them her ring and told them Giuseppe had proposed, they weren't surprised, but they were very excited for her.

"Oh, my God, that ring is beautiful!" Celeste said. "I'm jealous," she giggled, and Serafina blushed.

Serafina and her family spent a few minutes together dreaming up wedding ideas, and Serafina told them about the elegant Valentine's Day Ball at the Waldorf. After visiting with them for a while, Serafina knew there was something else she needed to do.

"I'm going over to the flower shop," she told them. "I have to go tell Miss Antoinette my exciting news!" she said as she headed out the door.

When Serafina walked through the door, she had a huge smile on her face. Miss Antoinette was standing behind the counter and looked up as she heard the door open.

"So?" Miss Antoinette said when she saw Serafina walk in. "Was it everything you dreamed of?" she asked.

"Oh, it was!" Serafina exclaimed. She walked over to the counter and held out her left hand, displaying her engagement ring.

"Oh my God! Serafina!" she said with excitement. "It is beautiful! I want to hear all about it," Miss Antoinette said. "Don't you leave out one thing," she said laughing.

Serafina giggled and blushed. She was in heaven, excited that Miss Antoinette wanted to hear her story.

"I'll make sure you have the most amazing flowers ever at the wedding," Miss Antoinette smiled.

"That I will, for sure," Serafina acknowledged. She grabbed Miss Antoinette's hand and led her into the back room so she could tell her all about her amazing night.

* * *

Two days later, Serafina was making Giuseppe his usual Monday night dinner. He loved her cooking. She always made him homemade gravy and pasta on Monday nights after work. He always joked that she knew the key to his heart was through his stomach and cooked such great food to ensure he continued to love her. It was 6:00 p.m. when Giuseppe finally walked through the door of his apartment.

"Hello, Princess," he called to her from the hallway.

"Hello, Sweetheart," she yelled from the kitchen.

* * *

Giuseppe was taking off his waders as Serafina walked into the dining room with a large bowl of pasta.

"How was your day?" she asked, leaning over and kissing him gently.

"I want to tell you something," he said. "Have a seat." He pulled out a chair at the table, and she sat down.

"What is it?" she said, sounding worried.

"I got the job!" he said excitedly.

"What? Oh, my God, baby. I'm so happy for you!" she said as she jumped out of her chair and hugged him.

"I leave the first week of March," he said.

"Wait … what?" she asked, looking confused and dismayed.

"I leave the first week of March," he said again. "It's only two weeks, Serafina."

"March holds the roughest seas, Giuseppe," she said, the worry in her voice written across her face.

"It will be okay," he said.

"I thought that season started in calmer waters," Serafina said, pacing across the room and back. "You said it was usually around the middle of April."

"Captain wants me to take a crew out early. I have to go across the sea to another port to help a crew out over there for two weeks. I will be fine," he said.

"No, Giuseppe. It is too dangerous. I won't lose you!" she cried.

"I have to go, Serafina, or I will lose the lead fisherman position," he said, trying to reason with her.

"No, it is way too dangerous. I forbid you to go," she said, angrily.

"You forbid me to go? This is my job, Serafina! I worked hard for this position! I'm a fisherman. This is what I do!" he yelled at her. Tears welled up in Serafina's eyes, and she started sobbing.

"What about me, Giuseppe? Is the money that important to you? More important than me?" she yelled back, feeling hurt.

"You knew I was a fisherman when you met me," he said, sternly. "I am going and that is the end of this discussion," he snapped at her.

"Well, *if* you come back, I won't be here waiting for you." she said sobbing, as tears streamed down her face. She took off her ring and threw it at his feet as she grabbed her satchel and headed towards the door.

"Good, then go!" Giuseppe yelled at her back. Tears ran down her face, practically blinding her as she slammed the door behind her.

Who does she think she is telling me I can't go? he thought stubbornly.

Serafina cried all the way back to the flower shop. The light was still on in the back room when she pulled up to the shop.

"What is the matter?" Miss Antoinette asked, seeing Serafina's red, swollen eyes and tear-stained cheeks when she walked through the door.

"We had a fight. He got the job, but they are making him go out to sea the first week in March!" she cried.

"Oh, my darling. That is tough, but Serafina, I told you about dating a fisherman," Miss Antoinette told her, reminding her of that day in the truck on the way home from the Waldorf.

"He had told me the season didn't start until the middle of April, but now he says his captain is sending him out early. The water is too rough! It's too dangerous." she cried.

"I know, dear. I know," Miss Antoinette said, hugging her and stroking her hair.

"I gave him back his ring. I told him I wouldn't marry him if he goes, she said, babbling on. "I love him. I don't want him to go. I can't lose him. He can stay in his senior fisherman position and still make good money, but he is choosing his money over me," she cried.

Miss Antoinette knew it wasn't as simple as that. "Oh, Serafina, honey. Give it a couple days. He will settle down. It was just a silly fight," she said, comforting her.

* * *

Three days passed, and Serafina hadn't heard a word from Giuseppe. She was sick to her stomach and worried.

Would he come back and apologize? Would he tell her she was more important than the money? Would he tell her he still loves her, and he didn't mean to tell her to go? She had so many questions.

She cried every day, all the while fighting the urge to reach out to him. She was trying to give him his space and time so he could come to his senses and realize he could never just let her walk away.

She tried to keep busy, and it helped that there were a lot of things going on. She had plenty of work at the flower shop. Celeste was graduating high school soon, and they were planning a graduation party for her. Her mother was going to be receiving an award for teacher of the year, and her father was busy in the shop and doing well with sales.

Things seemed to be going great for everyone else but her. The pain in her heart was unbearable. The silence was killing her, but somehow, she managed to press on. Her mother and Celeste kept telling her that men will sometimes walk away for a bit to cool down, but the ones who truly love you would never ever abandon you. She held onto that hope.

* * *

Giuseppe was also a mess. He couldn't sleep at night. He stayed home drinking whiskey from the bottle most nights to drown out the thoughts of Serafina. He laid in bed and held her ring in his hand, just staring at it. He hadn't showered or shaved in days since the fight. He continued to go to work while trying not to think about her, but it was impossible to get her off his mind. Serafina was the only thing he could think of. He felt guilty for hurting her. He couldn't erase the memory of watching the sweetest woman her ever met, the person he loved most in the world, cry in front of him while he just stood there.

Giuseppe hated himself for not just going over to the flower shop and telling Serafina how much he loved her and that he couldn't live without her. *Maybe she is better off without me,* he thought. *She deserves a man who would never let her walk out crying.* A man who wouldn't cause her heart pain like he did.

Serafina hadn't reached out to him at all. He thought maybe she would come back the next day and tell him she loved him.

He was destroyed over the whole mess, and he knew it was all his fault. He did make good money as a senior fisherman, and she was right. March is the most dangerous of times to set out to sea.

Was I just being selfish? he wondered. He called the dock and told the captain he was backing out of the position. He told him he had a family situation he needed to take care of.

"Giuseppe, you are the best man I got," Jake said. "I need a strong fisherman to run this job. I understand, though. If you change your mind let me know," Jake said as he said as he hung up the phone.

* * *

A week passed by and neither Serafina nor Giuseppe had reached out to talk to the other. They both wanted the other person to make the first move.

Serafina and Miss Antoinette had a lot of heart-to-heart talks, and Serafina was glad she had her as a wise friend who understood what she was going through the past week. Serafina was also prone to horrible crying spells. The simplest reminder of Giuseppe caused her tears to flow.

"Why doesn't he come for me? I don't understand. Was all of it a big lie?" she asked Antoinette one afternoon. "How do you love someone the way he loved me and then just let them go so easily?" she cried, sobbing into Miss Antoinette's motherly embrace.

"Give it some time, dear. Some men are stubborn and let their pride get in the way. He will come around. Don't chase him. He will come to you," Miss Antoinette advised her.

CHAPTER 6

~A moment too late~

GIUSEPPE WAS DUE TO SET SAIL THE NEXT DAY AT 1:00 P.M. HE had given Serafina almost a full two weeks, and he hadn't heard a word from her.

She hates me, he thought. *She said she wouldn't be there waiting for me, and she really walked away.*

Giuseppe was devastated. *She was my world*, he thought to himself. *If she isn't coming back, what do I have to lose*? he thought, so a couple days earlier he had called Jake and told him he was back on the lead.

Jake was ecstatic to hear the news. He knew Giuseppe was the best man for the job.

As he was packing his bag for his fishing boat, Giuseppe saw Serafina's ring sitting on his nightstand, and he walked over, picking it up. For the first time since the fight, he finally broke down and cried.

The tears cleared his head, and Giuseppe suddenly got an idea. He decided he was going to give it one more try with Serafina. He wrapped her ring in a box and wrote her a note that he tucked inside. He gathered up the courage and walked over to the small mailbox in front of the flower shop. He dropped the small, wrapped box labeled "Serafina" into the mailbox.

* * *

The following morning Miss Antoinette was running late to the flower shop, so she asked Serafina to get there early to open up for the day. Usually, Serafina would grab the mail from the box on the way in, but since it was early, and she was in a hurry, she decided to return for it later.

It was 10:00 a.m. on the dot when she opened the door to the flower shop, and there was a gentleman already standing there, waiting for the shop to open. She unlocked the door and ushered the man in and then headed behind the desk. The gentleman began to browse around the shop.

"I will be right with you, sir," Serafina said, as she ran into the back room to turn on the lights and put her bag down, then quickly ran back to the front of the store.

"How can I help you?" she asked him, out of breath from running around.

"I would like a dozen red, baby roses, please," he requested.

"Sure. Give me a minute, and I will wrap those up for you," she said.

She headed off to the back room and grabbed twelve flawless roses from the fridge. She tore off a large piece of clear cellophane and wrapped the roses up in it and tied it with a large, red satin ribbon and headed back out to the register.

"Well, these must be for someone very special," she said as she rang his order up.

"Oh yes, miss. I am setting sail today, and these are for my lady," he replied.

"Setting sail?" She questioned, the blood draining out of her face. She looked over at the calendar on the wall. It was March third.

"You work on the dock?" she asked.

"Yes, miss, I do," he replied.

"Who is your lead fisherman?" she asked prying, although she dreaded the answer.

"I'm not exactly sure, miss. I think someone said our lead backed out of the position. I mean, at least that was the talk around the docks. Captain was looking for a new lead," he told her.

A smile spread across Serafina's face at the news. He loved her! She knew he couldn't just leave without even coming to say goodbye. Her heart felt light for the first time in over three weeks.

"That will be fifty-seven euros," she said to the gentleman.

"Here you go," he said, handing her the money.

"Thank you, sir, and please be careful out there," she said to him.

"Thanks, miss," he said and walked out of the shop.

Serafina smiled and sighed with relief. *This all was just a silly fight,* she thought to herself. *After work, I am going to go over there and tell him how sorry I am, how much I love him, and that I can't live without him,* she thought to herself.

* * *

It was 12:30 p.m., and the boat was loading. The dock was a flurry of activity.

"Mario, those flowers for me?" Giuseppe teased him.

"Giuseppe, I thought you were off this position. What happened?" Mario asked.

"I'm back on. My girl left me. She hates me anyways, so figured I'd go," he said as he boarded the boat.

"Hey man, I thought you signed off this mission," Marco also asked Giuseppe.

"Back on. She left me," he told Marco.

"What? What happened?" Marco pried.

"She told me not to go because the sea was too dangerous right now, and we had a big fight about it. I backed out of the crew, but she never came back. I took her beautiful ring that I gave her on the best night of my life, and I wrapped it up in a box. I left her a note telling her if she showed up here by noon I would stay. I dropped it in the mailbox at her work last night," he told Marco.

Marco looked at his watch. "It's 12:45. Sorry, man," he said.

"Exactly," Giuseppe replied. "So, I am going. She has my ring and my heart, and I have nothing," he said as he headed back into the bunk area of the boat to drop his bags.

"Damn, man, that sucks," Marco said.

"Yup. Okay, guys, it's quarter to one, and we need to get this boat ready to sail," Giuseppe said.

* * *

Miss Antoinette walked through the door to the flower shop as Serafina was checking out a customer.

"Hey, Serafina, you forgot to grab the mail this morning, so I got it for you," Miss Antoinette said. "Oh, and by the way, look what came in the mail for you," she said as she waved the small box in front of Serafina's face.

"Oh my God," Serafina said as she grabbed the box, both excited and frightened about what it contained. She tore it open, and sure enough … it was her engagement ring. There was a piece of paper with a note tucked inside the box.

"Read it," Miss Antoinette said, anxiously.

"Serafina, I have been a fool to think I could ever live without you. I cannot sleep without holding you in my arms. I can't rest not knowing where you are or what you are doing. Losing you has been almost like a death to me. If you can find it in your heart to forgive a foolish man like me, meet me at the dock at noon.

"If you show up, I will not set sail. If you choose to stay away, then I want you to always have my ring. If I could give you my heart from my chest I would, my dearest Serafina. You will always be My Forever Valentine. Meet me at noon. I will be waiting.

Love Always,
Giuseppe"

"What? What time is it?" Serafina panicked.

"It's five minutes to one, Serafina," Miss Antoinette yelled. "Go. Run. You can still make it."

Serafina dashed towards the door and out onto the cobblestone street. She ran towards the wooden staircase to the dock. It seemed like forever by the time she made it up the stairs. There were people all over the dock—families saying goodbye, fisherman working.

"Ben! Ben!" she yelled out, running up to a big burly man who worked with Giuseppe.

"Serafina," he said. "You just missed Giuseppe." He just pulled out about five minutes ago.

"Nooo!!" She yelled as she pushed her way through the crowd to the end of the dock. Giuseppe's boat was already a good mile out. She cried hysterically as she watched the boat carrying her true love sail further and further away, approaching the horizon. Finally, she couldn't watch any longer.

Serafina ran to the wooden staircase on the dock, feeling as if her heart was going to explode from grief. She continued crying as she walked down the stairs and back to the flower shop. Miss Antoinette was checking out a customer at the front desk when she walked in.

"I missed him," she sobbed.

"Oh honey, when he comes back, go and see him. This whole silly mess will be over," Miss Antoinette said, encouraging her. "It's only two weeks, sweetheart. Let's just stay positive and wait on his return," she continued, hoping to help Serafina calm down.

"You're right," Serafina said, receiving a bit of comfort from Miss Antoinette's words. "I mean, after all, it's only a two-week trip," she said, reassuring herself.

Serafina put her ring back on, already planning on ways to surprise Giuseppe when he returned home. She was actually starting to see how silly she was for being so worried.

* * *

A week went by and the seas had been calmer than they had been in a very long time for March; nevertheless, Serafina and Miss Antoinette prayed every day for Giuseppe's safe return.

Serafina tried to keep herself as busy as possible to help the time go by quickly while Giuseppe was gone. She had dinner outings with Miss Antoinette and Vincenzo a couple of times, and that helped to pass the time. At dinner they talked about wedding plans and where Serafina and Giuseppe should go on their honeymoon. Miss Antoinette also threw around some ideas for centerpieces, bouquets, and wedding flowers in general.

* * *

It was week two since Giuseppe had been gone, and his boat was due to be back in just a few short days. Serafina couldn't wait to lie in his arms once again. She missed him terribly. It had been too long, and she just wanted to lay her head on his chest and listen to his heartbeat in her ear. She couldn't wait to tell him how much she had missed him.

Serafina thought it would be wildly romantic to meet Giuseppe's boat on the dock, holding a candlelit lantern. She would be his maiden waiting on her love to return in the night, just like in older times. She asked her father if he could make her a wooden lantern, and he agreed. He had been working on it in his free time for a couple days now.

"Serafina?" Rocco said as he knocked on her bedroom door early that Thursday morning. She opened her eyes and jumped out of bed, heading towards the door.

"Coming, Father," she called out as she opened the door. Her father was standing there with his hands behind his back.

"Serafina, I have a surprise for you," he said as he pulled the wooden lantern out from behind his back.

"Oh father, it is beautiful!" she exclaimed—and it truly was magnificent. The lantern was solid oak with a large silver handle and beautiful glass windows that surrounded a large, white pillar candle. There was a hinged door on the side of the lantern that locked shut with silver clasps. On the side of the lantern her father had carved, "May the light guide you home," into the wood. Serafina stared at the lantern in amazement and adoration.

"Do you really like it?" her father asked.

"I do, Father. I love it! Thank you so much," she said as she reached out and gave him a huge hug.

"It is 9:00 a.m., honey. You need to get ready for work. I'll let you get dressed," he said as he kissed her forehead gently. He handed her the beautiful wooden lantern and disappeared through the small bedroom doorway.

Serafina held up her lantern, admiring it for just how truly beautiful it was. She walked over to the nightstand next to her bed and set the lantern down, then quickly hurried off to shower and get dressed.

* * *

It was overcast that morning on the coast. It wasn't raining heavily, at least not yet, but it was misting. There was an eerie feeling in the air, and the thought of a storm possibly being ahead made Serafina's stomach uneasy.

She walked to the flower shop holding her satchel over her head to avoid getting her hair damp. She reached the door and unlocked it, heading directly towards the register to open up for the day.

Miss Antoinette practically blew through the door shortly after Serafina arrived. She had a worried look on her face as she looked at Serafina.

"It's just a little rain," Serafina said, looking back at Miss Antoinette, trying to downplay a possible storm brewing in the seas.

Miss Antoinette walked past Serafina and into the back room. She turned on the lights and the radio as she set up the supplies for the day's arrangements on the table.

While Miss Antoinette hurried around, Serafina stared out the glass window on the door of the flower shop. The wind was picking up, and the rain seemed a bit heavy and steadier.

Serafina tried to distract herself from the negative thoughts, but despite her best efforts, she couldn't help noticing they were taking over her mind. Tears welled in her eyes as she watched the rain and wind. Serafina gathered her emotions and walked into the back room to help Miss Antoinette.

By the time another hour went by, you could hear the wind whistling through the back door of the shop. Serafina and Miss Antoinette looked at each other a couple times with worried expressions, but neither one of them said a word. Serafina was cutting ribbon and Miss Antoinette was gathering more flowers from the fridge when the announcement came over the radio.

"There is a tropical cyclone warning in effect for the Amalfi coast. Inhabitants of the coast are encouraged to move further inland, board up windows, and remain on alert for further news and instructions," the radio DJ warned.

"What did he say?" Serafina looked alarmed. "A cyclone?" she said, growing even more frightened as the words escaped her lips.

"It's just a warning," Miss Antoinette said, trying to soothe Serafina. "Giuseppe is smart. He is an experienced sailor and knows the ins and outs of the boats he works on. He will be just fine," but Miss Antoinette knew deep down that the seas in March were no place for unskilled fisherman, or those as young as Giuseppe. The threat of a cyclone off this coast was nothing short of dangerous, and they both knew that Giuseppe could be in the middle of the storm.

Two hours passed by, and the weather outside was getting worse. The wind had picked up speed, the rain was whipping against the windows, and the sky was a dark shade of gray. Suddenly another announcer came across the radio.

"There is a state of emergency in effect for all of the Amalfi Coast. Inhabitants of the coast are ordered to evacuate and travel inland as of 2:00 p.m. today," the radio station announced.

"Come on, Serafina, we need to board up the door and windows and get out of here," Miss Antoinette said, interrupting Serafina's reverie as she walked over to the closet and pulled out the plywood boards she kept on hand for storms.

Serafina walked over and helped Miss Antoinette carry the boards. The two of then quickly nailed the boards to the store's windows and front door.

"Serafina, you need to go home. You have to evacuate the coast with your family," Miss Antoinette said.

"No! I can't leave," Serafina cried. "I have to wait for Giuseppe."

"You have no choice. Serafina. You must go," Miss Antoinette ordered. She packed up the truck to get ready to leave.

"I am going to my sister's house in Rome for a few days," Miss Antoinette said as she hopped into the driver seat of the truck.

"Serafina! Come, let's go!" she heard her father call out from down the street, his voice barely audible over the sound of the wind.

Serafina ran down the cobblestone walk as the wind and rain whipped against her skin.

"Get in the car, Serafina! We are going to Nonna's house in Tuscany to ride out the storm," Rocco said.

"I can't go! Giuseppe is out there in the water," Serafina cried. "His boat is just off the coast by now. He is due to arrive in only a day's time," she cried to her father.

"Serafina! Get in this car, now!" her father yelled at her. The wind was blowing so hard they had to hold on to the car's doors to steady themselves.

"God, please," she cried out. "Please God, keep my Giuseppe safe," she begged, looking up at the foreboding sky. She closed her eyes and got into the backseat of the car next to Celeste. As her father drove off, Serafina sobbed, looking back through the car window at the dock until it was out of sight, while tears streamed from her emerald eyes down her face.

CHAPTER 7

~Shipwrecked~

"GIUSEPPE, THE WATER IS COMING OVER THE DECK!" MARIO yelled into the cabin of the fishing boat. The boat was being tossed around mercilessly by the crashing tide.

"We need to steer out of this," Giuseppe instructed one of his men at the wheel.

"I'm trying, but the force is too strong. We will be sure to capsize if I turn this wheel too sharply," the fisherman yelled back.

Giuseppe met Mario out on the front deck of the boat. "Are all the nets in?" Giuseppe yelled to the men on deck.

"Yes, we pulled the last of them up a few minutes ago," Mario yelled as he held onto the mast of the boat. The waves were crashing over the railings on both sides of the boat, and it was rocking viciously from side to side.

"We are only a couple days away from returning home," Giuseppe said to the men on deck. "If I can steer further south, we may be able to wait out the storm in calmer seas. Everyone hunker down tight. I am going to steer this boat around and try to head south out of this," he yelled over the crashing of the waves hitting the deck.

The wind was whipping water across the boat and the men, all dressed in yellow rain gear, were trying to protect their faces from the pounding rain. They held onto the mast and planted their feet to the deck, steadying themselves for the shift. Giuseppe headed back into the boat's cabin.

"I'm taking the wheel," he shouted to the fisherman steering the boat, over the sound of the storm.

"But, sir!" the man responded with fear in his eyes, worried that Giuseppe didn't understand what a sharp turn in these seas could cause. "We could capsize," the fisherman yelled to him.

"Do you have any better ideas?" Giuseppe asked. "Hunker down!" he yelled at him.

Giuseppe grabbed the wheel and slowly turned it a sharp left. The boat rocked so hard to the left that the men slid down the deck and items that weren't fastened down went flying over the side of the boat into the water. The boat was creaking from the waves and weight of the water that had spilled onto the deck.

"There's a hole in the deck!" Mario yelled in panic. The boat turned back upright and quickly swung sharply to the right. The pull of the ocean was so strong it pushed the boat all the way to the right. The port side of the boat was in the air and touching the water. The men were yelling orders to one another, their voices full of fear.

"Sir—" the young fisherman said to Giuseppe with a look of terror on his face.

"Marco, It looks like we may not make it out of this alive," Giuseppe said. As he said those words, his thoughts immediately went to Serafina in that moment—how he had let her down, how he was too stubborn to just go make things right with her—and now her worst nightmares were about to become a reality. His feelings of remorse outweighed his fear.

The lights inside the cabin of the boat were flickering, the deck was flooding with water, and the hull was beginning to break apart. Mario came running into the cabin.

"Look!" he yelled. Giuseppe and the young sailor looked out the window of the cabin to see a gigantic wave standing about ten feet tall in front of the boat. There was an enormous crash … and everything went black.

* * *

The water was cold and dark. The waves were crashing, and the rain was pounding hard against the ocean as Giuseppe looked back at the wreckage. The boat was sinking as he watched helplessly. He was trying to catch his breath, but he kept being pulled under by the rough water.

"Giuseppe," he heard a man cry out. He looked around frantically as he was being pulled under and coming back up.

"Mario!" he yelled out. He spotted Mario struggling in the water just several feet away.

Giuseppe saw a large piece of wood from the boat's deck floating next to him. He grabbed onto it and pulled himself up on his stomach.

"Mario, swim!" Giuseppe yelled. "Swim over here!" He watched Mario struggling to stay above water.

Giuseppe started paddling with his hands as fast as he could, trying to fight against the rough waves. He finally made it over to Mario despite the force of the water working against him. He grabbed Mario's yellow jacket from under the water and pulled him up onto the large wooden plank, alongside him.

"Whatever you do, you hold on tight. Do not let go," Giuseppe instructed.

* * *

The next morning the sea was calm, and the sun was shining a beautiful reflection on the water as Giuseppe opened his eyes. It was like waking up from a nightmare. Mario was lying on the wooden plank next to him.

"Mario, wake up," Giuseppe said as he patted Mario on the back.

"Ughhh," Mario groaned.

They were floating somewhere in the middle of the ocean. Their boat and the men were all gone. Giuseppe stared off into the ocean in disbelief. Mario sat up and looked at Giuseppe.

"Well, this is just great," he said looking out at the ocean stretching to the horizon in every direction.

"Mm-hmm…" Giuseppe replied, speechless.

CHAPTER 8

~*Love Lost At Sea*~

THREE DAYS AT NONNA'S IN TUSCANY WERE PURE TORTURE for Serafina. The minutes ticked by slowly, and Serafina felt like a prisoner, desperate to get home and find out about Giuseppe's boat but unable to do so.

Her father decided to spend a couple extra days with Nonna, since they really didn't get to see her very often. The news said the storm had ended two days ago, but the town of Midori was in pretty bad shape.

Serafina cried daily, worrying herself sick over Giuseppe. Where was he? Did his boat come back in? Was he looking for her? All these questions swirled around in her mind, driving her mad with trepidation. She had to share the extra bedroom downstairs at Nonna's house with Celeste, and she was starting to grow tired of not having her own space to cry in peace.

Father, can we please head back today?" Serafina asked him at breakfast. "I love spending time with Nonna, don't get me wrong, but I have to get back to Giuseppe," she pleaded with him, her eyes overflowing with sadness.

"We will leave in the morning, Serafina. If Giuseppe was out during the storm, he probably had to move to calmer waters, so his return would certainly have been delayed, anyways," her father said, trying to reassure her that everything would be okay.

* * *

Serafina and Celeste spent the day picking grapes in the vineyard, which helped the time go by a bit more quickly. Nonna made her own wine, and it was always the girls' job to go and collect the grapes for her when they visited.

When the girls were little, the best part about the vineyard was when Nonna would let them take off their shoes and stomp the grapes. They would giggle and smoosh their feet into the purple mush until their feet were as purple as the grapes. It was a wonderful memory of their summers in Tuscany with Nonna that she and Celeste shared.

It was hot in the vineyard, and as there was no shade, the full sun beat down on them. Serafina thought about Giuseppe and how much she missed him as she walked among the vines picking grapes. She thought about how stubborn she was being by not just going to see him before he left, regardless of their differences. Now she would give anything to hug him and hold him close to her. She prayed that he would still be open to reconciling when he got back. Her memories of him and the longing she felt for him were almost too much for her heart to bear.

* * *

It was dinnertime and Nonna had made homemade ravioli and meatballs, and the aroma permeated the entire house. Nonna was a fantastic cook, and the meals she prepared were always delicious. Bottles of her homemade red wine and fresh vegetable salad made with produce harvested from her garden complemented the savory Tuscan meal.

As Serafina enjoyed her dinner, she told Nonna all about Giuseppe. Nonna smiled and her eyes sparkled as Serafina told her about their romantic night at the Waldorf's Valentine's Day Ball when Giuseppe proposed.

Nonna was excited to learn that there may be an upcoming wedding in the family. She told Serafina she wanted to provide a bottle of her homemade wine for each table at the wedding reception.

Celeste told Nonna about graduation and how she was looking into possibly attending college in the United States. Colette shared stories about her children at school, and Rocco told Nonna he would fix a couple planks on the wooden fence out in the vineyard for her before they left in the morning. With the food, the wine, and the conversation, it was a wonderful night with the family. The only thing missing was Giuseppe, Serafina thought to herself as she grabbed her heart, feeling a tightness in her chest. The sadness and heartbreak of missing him were becoming a physical ache.

That evening Serafina sat out at the picnic table on Nonna's concrete patio that overlooked her vineyard behind her house, enjoying the beauty of the Tuscan countryside as the sun was setting. Small strings of lights with decorative metal grapevines wrapped around them adorned the trellis above the patio, adding to the Tuscan charm and making Serafina miss Giuseppe even more.

Rocco was fixing some of Nonna's fence as Colette helped Nonna bring out some fresh gelato and cheesecake for dessert. Aside from her family, the only audible evening sounds in the Tuscan countryside around them were of the crickets and tree frogs.

Serafina took a deep breath as she looked up into the sky at the stars. She thought of Giuseppe and dreamed of their wedding day. She hoped he was looking up at the same stars she was and that for a moment he knew they were together under the very same sky.

* * *

Morning came and Rocco packed the car while the girls were saying their goodbyes to Nonna. Serafina hugged Nonna and bid her a quick goodbye, then ran to the car and hopped into the backseat, anxiously waiting to leave. She was eager to get back to the coast as fast as she could and hopefully be reunited with Giuseppe. It was about a three-hour drive back to Midori from Nonna's place in Tuscany.

Serafina watched through the car window as Celeste and Colette hugged Nonna, one by one. They walked towards the car and Celeste hopped in the backseat next to Serafina. Colette got in the passenger seat as Rocco kissed and hugged Nonna goodbye. Finally, Rocco walked over to the car and got in the driver's seat. Nonna waved as they pulled out and headed towards home.

The long car ride seemed unending, and Serafina stared out the window, anxiously wondering if Giuseppe would be there when they got back. About two hours into the ride she finally fell asleep.

"We are here," Rocco said as he pulled onto their street in Midori. Serafina opened her eyes and stretched as she looked out the window. Midori had been hit hard by the storm. The stores had siding hanging from them, and windows were broken. There was debris and trash scattered on the streets and in front of homes and storefronts. *It looks awful*, she thought as they drove to their apartment, but Midori was still a beautiful sight for her to see.

"I hope the shop is okay," Rocco said, sounding worried as he looked at the disaster the storm had left in its wake. When they pulled up in front of the shop, Serafina's father got out and looked around, assessing the damage to the shop.

"Well, it looks like I am going to have to replace the door and a few of the wooden steps heading upstairs, but for the most part it seems we got lucky," he said.

Serafina hopped out of the backseat of the car. "I am going to the docks," she yelled as she ran off to the wooden staircase off Via del Gelso.

When she reached the staircase, she discovered that some of the boards were broken, so she had to step over them while she climbed the stairs. The dock was torn up a bit and the wooden railing at its edge was broken. She looked around to see if she spotted Giuseppe anywhere.

"Ben!" she yelled out as she ran over to him on the other end of the dock. "Ben!" she cried out again as she got closer to him.

"Serafina," he replied.

"Ben? Where is Giuseppe?" she asked. Ben looked at her with a saddened face.

"What is it, Ben? Where is he?" she asked a bit harshly and looked at him sternly, almost demanding an answer.

"His boat was due to come in a day ago. Serafina, listen—" he said.

"No, Ben," she said, angrily cutting him off. "No!" she yelled as she pushed him in his chest, sending him rocking back on his feet a bit and nearly losing his balance. Then she ran off towards the staircase crying.

"He can still come back," Ben yelled across the deck at her as she ran off down the stairs.

Serafina sobbed uncontrollably as she ran back home. Her father was outside the store taking the boards off the door when she ran straight into his arms.

"He is gone, Father. His boat never came in," she cried.

"Serafina, it is still so soon after the storm, sweetheart. He can still come back. It will be okay. Have hope, darling," her father said, trying to comfort her.

* * *

It was a Friday morning. Serafina got up out of bed and looked over at her lantern on the nightstand. She picked it up and studied it carefully, shedding a couple tears as she put it back in its spot on the nightstand before hurrying out of her room. She made her way out to the kitchen where her mother was cooking French toast for breakfast, and she had a bowl of fresh fruit on the counter.

"Good morning, Mother," Serafina said as she walked over to the cabinet and grabbed a plate.

"Good Morning, Serafina," Colette said. "French toast?" she asked.

"Yes, please," she replied.

Colette grabbed a slice of toast out of the pan and placed it on her plate. Serafina scooped some fruit onto her plate and grabbed a fork from the drawers. She walked over to the kitchen table where Celeste was sitting and writing a paper for school while eating her breakfast.

"Are you working today?" Colette asked Serafina.

"I think so. I am going to go over to the flower shop after I take a shower and see if Miss Antoinette is back and how her shop weathered the storm," she replied.

Serafina ate her breakfast in a hurry and walked her plate over to the sink. She kissed her mother, thanked her for breakfast and headed down the hallway to the bathroom.

The water at their house in Midori always heated up to a really hot temperature, and it felt good on her skin. The past few days they had to shower from the well water in the countryside, and the water just didn't get quite as hot as she liked.

The steam filled the bathroom as Serafina slipped off her nightgown and got into the shower. She let the water wash over her head and grabbed her sunflower shampoo off the tiny shelf as she lathered it into her locks. The scent of her shampoo took her thoughts back to Giuseppe, and it brought tears to her eyes. He always loved the smell of her hair. She started sobbing as the thoughts of him never coming back started to set in once again. She remembered what her father told her about him possibly being delayed because of the storm. She clung to that hope and pulled herself together, trying to turn the negative thoughts around.

She washed up and toweled off. She headed back to her bedroom and grabbed a sundress from her closet, put on her undergarments, and slid her dress over her head. She combed her damp hair and tied it back with a black rubber band, then slipped on her sandals and grabbed her satchel as she headed out the door.

The weather was warm, and the sky was a baby blue hue, reminding her of Giuseppe's beautiful eyes. Why did everything seem to remind her of him?

Store owners were outside cleaning debris off their lawns and sidewalks. Some were taking down the boards from their doors and windows. Most of the stores hadn't reopened yet since the storm hit.

Serafina walked over to the flower shop. Miss Antoinette was out front of the shop putting her sign back up. The storm had torn it straight from its chains. The sight of Miss Antoinette warmed Serafina's heart.

"Looks like that storm hit us pretty good, huh?" Mr. Bioni from the dry cleaners across the way yelled over to Antoinette. "

Yes, indeed," Miss Antoinette responded as she fastened the sign back to the post. Serafina walked up to Miss Antoinette and folded her into a much-needed hug.

"Serafina," Miss Antoinette said gently, hugging her back then trying to get a look into Serafina's eyes as she pulled away.

"No," Serafina knew what Miss Antoinette was asking and shook her head, trying to fight off tears.

"Oh, honey. Listen, maybe they stayed off the coast because of the storm. We need to stay positive, okay?" she said as hugged Serafina tightly once again. Serafina allowed herself to collapse into Miss Antoinette, as she sobbed into her shoulder.

* * *

Days passed by. Serafina waited on the dock every night for Giuseppe's boat to come in, but it never did. Her heart grew heavier and heavier with every passing day.

She tried to immerse herself in work most of the time to help get through the days. Every night she grabbed her lantern off her nightstand and climbed the wooden staircase to the dock, where she would sit on the edge of the dock overlooking the water and wait.

A few of the guys who worked with Giuseppe on the docks would come by and make small talk. They knew of her heartbreak. They kept telling her to stay positive, even though most of them knew it had been way too long with no radio communication. The reality was that if they weren't shipwrecked, they had probably starved to death from no food or water by now.

It was early April, and the seas were a lot calmer. Boats had been coming in and out if the port regularly. Serafina was still trying to remain hopeful that maybe Giuseppe had waited the rough seas out somewhere and couldn't get communication home.

Her birthday was coming up at the end of April, and she would be turning eighteen. Giuseppe had promised her that he would have a party for her birthday and maybe they would even go on a small holiday to the United States to meet his parents afterward. Serafina decided she was holding him to his promise. She wore his ring and had never taken it off since she received it in the mail the day his boat sailed off, nearly three weeks ago now. She looked at the ring every chance she had.

"Will you wear my heart?" she remembered Giuseppe always saying to her about the ring that symbolized his love for her.

"Every day," she always responded, and whenever she looked at her ring, she still said those words to him, although not aloud, hoping they would reach his thoughts across the sea, and that her love would bring him home safely.

* * *

It was busy at the flower shop as Easter was approaching. The residents of Midori were eager to welcome spring with beautiful baskets and arrangements of flowers, and orders were pouring in.

Springtime also held a lot of celebrations like baby showers, bridal showers, and weddings. There was plenty enough work to keep her busy at the flower shop and help keep her mind occupied as the weeks passed with no word from Giuseppe.

Most days, she thought of him all day long, but sometimes the pain of his absence was just too heavy to bear, and she would break down in tears at random times during the day. She was so grateful for her friendship with Miss Antoinette, who would hug her and try to give her some encouraging words, but even she was beginning to lose hope for Giuseppe's return, and her heart was also hurt by his loss.

Giuseppe was a great friend to Miss Antoinette, and she had gotten into the habit of making baskets of flowers and treats for the fishermen's kids and taking them to the dock in the evenings. She continued that tradition, hoping for some news of Giuseppe she could take back to Serafina.

CHAPTER 9

~Message in a Bottle~

IT WAS EASTER DAY, AND SERAFINA'S FAMILY WAS GOING TO BE having dinner around 5:00 p.m. The savory aroma of the meal filled the air throughout the home. Colette was preparing a large honey ham, baked potatoes, broccoli, and candied yams. Although she liked the local Italian cuisine, she still preferred a traditional American Easter dinner to remind her of home. A bottle of Nonna's Italian red wine also sat on the table, though, waiting to add a bit of Italy to the meal. Nonna always packed a couple boxes containing bottles of her homemade wine into the back of the car when she left Tuscany to join Serafina's family for Easter.

Serafina had brought home some pretty floral centerpieces that were left over from an Easter event she and Miss Antoinette put together. She placed one in the middle of the dinner table, accenting the already elegant table and adding the distinct fragrance of lilies, roses, and alstroemeria to the air.

As they all sat down to dinner, the table was full of family, food, love, and laughter. Serafina was already really missing Giuseppe, especially today, and the festivities of the holiday dinner made her feel her heartache more acutely.

Rocco had finished a couple glasses of Nonna's wine and was pouring himself another.

"Can I have a glass?" she asked her father.

"Sure," he said, pouring her a glass and handing it to her.

"Mmm," she said, closing her eyes as she took a sip, feeling the wine instantly beginning to relax her, exactly the therapeutic effect she was hoping for.

"Nonna makes the best wine," her father said, smiling and laughing in agreement, feeling the similar influence of the spirits he had been enjoying throughout dinner.

Although it was acceptable for teenagers in Italy to drink wine with their families, Serafina wasn't much of a drinker, but today she made an exception. After a glass of wine, she noticed that for the first time in weeks she was joking and laughing with Celeste and her mother. She was actually able to smile as the wine took the edge off her heartache, if even just for a little while.

* * *

Later that night, Serafina snuck into the pantry closet and grabbed an armful of bottles of Nonna's wine. She ran to her bedroom and stashed them under her bed, then popped the cork on one. As she took a swig right from the bottle, she noticed the sketch she had drawn of Giuseppe sticking out from underneath her bed. She grabbed it and laid across her bed, smoothing out the sketch in front of her. She touched the sketch lovingly, and as she looked at Giuseppe's shaded blue eyes, her heart felt a sinking, dull ache.

She grabbed her satchel and took out her notebook, then grabbed her pen from the satchel, continuing to drink wine as she wrote:

My dearest love,

> *My body misses your warm embrace. My eyes miss looking into those handsome blue eyes of yours. My heart is missing its home. My soul is missing its song. Days and nights without you by my side are so very long and so very lonely. My love for you cannot be undone. I am forever yours. You are the only man who will ever sing to my soul. You were my greatest love story. Please my love, if you get this message, come home to me. I cannot carry this pain of your absence much longer. I love you always and forever.*

> *Serafina*

She pulled the notebook page out of the leather binding, then reached for the wine bottle and gulped down the last bit of red wine from it. She rolled up the paper and slid it inside the bottle before corking it shut. She grabbed the lantern her father made her off the nightstand, lit the candle inside, and headed out of her bedroom towards the door.

She walked out into the night, down Via del Gelso, towards the jetty in front of the Waldorf. She climbed up onto the large black rocks and tossed the bottle as far as she could out into the dark water of the sea, wishing for her message to reach Giuseppe. She held up the wooden lantern in hopes that her true love would see its light and follow it back home.

* * *

Throughout the following days, Serafina adopted a new routine. She worked at the flower shop during the day and found herself lost in a bottle of red wine each night. While she drank the wine, she wrote messages to Giuseppe, sealing them in the empty wine bottle before making her way down to the jetty to toss her messages into the water and shine her lantern across the sea.

* * *

On April twenty seventh, Serafina turned eighteen. The weather was sunny and warm on the coast that day.

It had been six weeks since the storm that changed her life and almost two months since her horrible fight with Giuseppe. Losing Giuseppe devastated Serafina, and it was a struggle to get through each day with her broken heart.

Today was especially difficult for Serafina because she and Giuseppe had planned on celebrating her birthday together. They should be getting ready to fly to the United States so she could meet his parents. They should be planning their wedding. Instead, she had no idea whether he was even alive or dead. Far from being a happy day, her birthday was filled with sadness, and her tears flowed most of the day, heavily at times.

Rocco and Colette did the best they could to cheer Serafina up and ease her sorrow. Colette baked a cake, and they invited Miss Antoinette and Vincenzo, some of Serafina's favorite people, to come and celebrate at their home. Serafina didn't feel like there was much to celebrate, but she appreciated everyone's efforts, so she put on a brave face and smiled anyway for the people she loved.

* * *

That night after the guests left the house, Serafina escaped to the solitude of her bedroom. She pulled out a bottle of wine and began to numb her pain. She sprawled across her bed as usual, pulled out her notebook, and began to write:

My Beloved,

> *Your absence is felt in every tiny spot of my being. I push through my days with only thoughts of you. The evening hours bring the memories of you back in a crushing blow to my heart. I drown my pain in the red wine I drink. The music keeps me alive as I get lost in the lyrics of our love. Last night it was as if I could feel you holding me as I leaned against the table in the small back room of the flower shop. It brought tears to my eyes as I heard a faint whisper in my ear. I swore I heard you say, "It's okay." It was ever so comforting and peaceful. I long for the day when I can feel you again. I long for the day I can look into your blue eyes once more. I long for the day you return home to me.*

> *Love always, Serafina*

After finishing the letter, Serafina sipped down the last bit of wine in the bottle and slid the note inside. She corked it shut and grabbed her lantern from her nightstand, once again. She headed off to the jetty and climbed the familiar black rocks as she tossed the bottle into the ocean and held the lantern out across the water to her beloved Giuseppe.

* * *

Serafina spent the next couple weeks working as much as she could. She even picked up some extra hours at the flower shop in the evenings. That worked out well for Miss Antoinette, since it allowed her to a spend more evenings with Vincenzo.

Summer was approaching soon, and Serafina couldn't believe how much had changed since that day she met Giuseppe on the street just a few months earlier. The memories made her extremely happy, yet devastatingly sad all at the same time. She wasn't sleeping well, and the sleepless nights seemed to get longer and longer. Her heart was shattered in a million pieces, and there was nothing she could do to bring Giuseppe back. On top of losing him, she felt guilty for letting him leave without knowing she didn't mean the things she had said to him the night of their fateful fight.

* * *

Serafina sat in the back of the flower shop one night after putting together her orders for the following day. She had her bottle of wine with her as she worked. She found comfort in its ability to take away the sharp rawness of her grief. She pulled out her notebook from her satchel and wrote:

My Beloved,

> *There is nothing quite like the feeling of grief. The unending sadness, the rawness of pain that I feel at the mere thought of the tremendous loss of you. The great black abyss that time never seems to heal. The ache to reach out for your touch. The urge to just see your face once more. The subtle way that just one thought can destroy me even on my best day. The*

memories that leave me a sobbing mess of tears. Grieving is
messy, painful, soul shattering, and unending. I never knew of
the pain that death and loss could carry in its wake. It is even
harder that I am grieving a man when I don't even know if he
is dead or alive.

Please my love, find your way back home to me. I will give
you my heart from my chest. I will give you my last breath, my
love. Just come back and ease my unending heartbreak.

Love forever,
Serafina

She tore out the page from her notebook and sipped the rest of the wine. Then she continued her familiar ritual. She shoved the note into the bottle and corked it, gathered her things and lit her lantern she always took with her. She turned off the lights to the flower shop and locked the door behind her. She walked down to the jetty, climbed the slippery black rocks, and tossed the bottle off into the tide as she held the lantern in her outstretched hand, up towards the sky and over the dark waters.

* * *

It was July and the tourist season was in full swing. Tourists were buzzing all around the village once again.

The busy time of the year for weddings, graduations and other celebrations was also upon them at the flower shop. Celeste had been coming by the shop to help out sometimes since she had graduated from secondary school, the Italian equivalent of high school. Her extra set of hands was a welcome addition to Miss Antoinette's at such a busy time. Now that the tourists were back, Rocco really missed Serafina's help around his shop.

Fortunately, he had found a young apprentice who was giving him a hand and who enjoyed learning his woodworking craft, since the flower business consumed most of Serafina's time. She had discovered a love for working with flowers. She enjoyed creating beautiful arrangements from the various flowers and seeing the joy her work brought to others on their special occasions.

The flower shop was the only thing that brought her pleasure these last eight months. Miss Antoinette had even talked to her about possibly taking over the shop once she and Vincenzo retired to travel the world.

* * *

It was the fourth of July, and the coast was swamped with tourists. Midori held a festival this week each year to celebrate St. Elizabeth of Portugal, their town's patron saint, and visiting Americans took the opportunity to celebrate their Independence Day.

The town had an annual firework display off the dock for this occasion every year. People started packing into the town early to get a good spot to watch them. The shop was closing early for one of the biggest social celebrations of the year.

"Do you want to come down to see the fireworks with Vincenzo and I tonight?" Miss Antoinette asked.

"No, thanks. I think I will close up here, and maybe I'll take a walk down by the water later on," Serafina said with a smile.

"Okay, honey," Miss Antoinette said as she gathered her things to leave.

* * *

As soon as Miss Antoinette departed, Serafina pulled out her bottle of wine and turned up the radio that played the latest Italian love songs. She drank the wine as she pulled out her notebook from her satchel.

My Beloved,

It has been eight long months since I felt the presence of your safe embrace and your soul. The pain of your absence has devastated me to my very core. I have never experienced such anguish in my entire life. The tears flow uncontrollably at the thought of you never returning. The triggers of abandonment all rise to the surface. Days of longing to feel the relief in your embrace. They say time heals all wounds, so how is it that with every minute, every second, and every day that passes, my love and longing for you only grow stronger? My soul longs for you. There is a never-ending deep hole in my heart. A hole that only seems to get bigger as I shed the tears of longing and pain, of my heart missing its home. Please find your way back home to me, my love. I am waiting here for you. I have been waiting every night since you left. I will continue to wait until we are one again. Follow the light home to me, my love.

Love Always,
Serafina

* * *

That night Serafina made her way down to the jetty with her bottle and her lantern once again. As she stood on the jetty, she could see fireworks off in the distance and hear the loud booms from the fire crackers being set off. She tossed the bottle into the ocean and held out the lantern.

CHAPTER 10

~ A new Hope for Love ~

"HEY, MARIO DID YOU FIND ANY KIND OF MESH MATERIAL IN the woods back there?" Giuseppe asked.

"No, man, there is nothing to make a sail out of. I have been searching for days to find something," he replied.

"This is bullshit," Giuseppe, said frustrated. "We have been on this island now for months. The boat is finally almost ready, and we can't find a sail," he said in anger as he sat down in the sand next to the makeshift boat crafted from wood and leaves. The large plank of wood from their wrecked fishing boat that they drifted in on served as the flooring and they had built on that.

Giuseppe was thankful he had been a Boy Scout back in the United States when he was a child. During his time as a Scout he learned how to make tools from wood, and he learned a lot of survival skills. Those skills he learned years ago served him well and had kept Mario and him alive this long.

The two men had built a small shack on the edge of the island, and they had found a spring of fresh water. They built a campfire pit from rocks where they could cook food and boil water for drinking.

They hunted for snakes and small rodents for food as well as fish they would catch from the ocean. They had eaten things they never would have imagined, but it had kept them alive, and Giuseppe thought on more than one occasion how it would have made his Boy Scout leader proud. They had been on the island for months, and they hadn't spotted one boat or plane.

"I wish I had a way to get word back to the coast that we are alive," Mario said. "My lady probably thinks I am dead."

Giuseppe's thoughts turned to Serafina, and his heart ached in pain. He missed her so much. "Why didn't I listen to Serafina? I was such a fool … such a complete idiot! I was so hard-headed that I let the best thing in my life get away. She didn't want me to come on this fishing trip. She thought it was too dangerous, but I let my pride get in the way, and now look where I am," he said to Mario with tears in his eyes.

"She was so beautiful. I am sure she has moved on by now. She told me to keep the ring. She said if I went to not look back, and now that I am gone, she has probably already long since forgotten me. I love her with all my heart." Giuseppe told Mario.

"Well, then what are we doing sitting here? Let's get to building the rest of this boat," Mario said as he got up. Giuseppe stood up and followed behind him.

Giuseppe and Mario worked endlessly, day and night, cutting tree limbs and gathering leaves and rocks to make a hatch for the boat. Mario even made a set of wooden paddles one night when he couldn't sleep. The two men were determined to get off that island and get home.

Surviving on the island was difficult enough. Making the boat in addition was a grueling task. Giuseppe wanted to give up many times as the days passed, but the memory of Serafina's face in his mind kept him hopeful when all seemed lost.

Giuseppe and Mario had become close as they worked together each day and shared many stories of their lives while sitting around their camp-fire night after night. Talking about home made getting back seem more like a reality ... and a possibility.

Mario told Giuseppe all about his lady, Maria, and how she had told him just days before they left that she was expecting a baby. She would be due to have the baby soon, and Mario was determined to get back home to her before that. He didn't want to miss the birth of his baby.

* * *

The days were long and tiresome, but finally the boat was almost finished. The men celebrated their success by feasting on a large fish they had caught just off the shoreline.

"This should hopefully sail us straight on out—back towards the coast. Let's hope," Giuseppe said as he pointed at the somewhat sad-look-ing, makeshift boat.

"The water is a bit rough in one area to the northeast of here, but if we reinforce the bottom of the boat, we should be able to make it through." Giuseppe told Mario.

"Well then let's go get some more wood and get to work," Mario said. He picked up the handmade axe, and they headed off into the woods.

* * *

Giuseppe was cutting a large tree branch when he had a sudden pain in his chest. He felt short of breath and had to stop and take a seat on the ground.

"Are you ok?" Mario asked, worried.

"Yea, I think so. Just tired," Giuseppe replied, placing his hand over his heart. The truth was he had been having this pain for months now, but he just kept pushing through. It started with an occasional dull ache in the middle of his chest, and at first, he thought it was just the heartbreak over missing Serafina, but it started becoming more frequent and intense throughout the past week. He was also beginning to have trouble breathing, often finding himself unexpectedly short of breath. He thought maybe it was caused by malnutrition or some vitamins he was lacking, so he shrugged it off and continued working.

* * *

It was a cold misty morning on the small island. The water was freezing cold as they washed their faces in it trying to wake up enough to survive the voyage back home.

"Giuseppe! Look!" Mario said in excitement as he pointed towards a red object floating just out of his reach. He quickly walked out into the water far enough to lean out and grab it. It looked to be an old sail that may have been torn off a boat.

"It's a sail!" Mario yelled out as he lifted it out of the cold water.

"Bring it here," Giuseppe called out to him. Mario headed back to shore with the wet red sail in hand.

"Let's dry this out," Giuseppe said as he took it from Mario and stretched it out to inspect it for holes. Thankfully, it was intact. They both grabbed an end and took it to the tree line off the shore, studying it in disbelief.

"Let's drape it over the branches to dry," Giuseppe said. The two men unfolded the red sail and stretched it across two trees in a hammock-like manner.

Hours passed by as they put the final touches onto the wooden planks and tied up the ends with strings from their shoelaces and other articles of clothing they had on them. When the sail was fully dry, Giuseppe and Mario attached it to their boat, and they prepared to set sail in hopes of reaching the coast of Italy.

"You ready?" Mario asked Giuseppe eagerly.

"Ready as I could ever be," Giuseppe replied nervously, once again grabbing at his chest as he felt the now-familiar ache calling for attention. He shrugged it off as anxiety about their upcoming adventure and walked over to the water's edge to meet Mario. The two of them climbed up onto the large makeshift boat, and they each grabbed a paddle.

Mario had begun to notice the physical changes in Giuseppe and saw him clutch his chest. "Are you sure you're okay?" he asked again, worried. "If you need to rest a bit we can wait," Mario said to him.

"I am fine. I am not waiting a minute longer to get off this island," Giuseppe replied, downplaying the situation.

"Ok then," Mario said. They placed the paddles in the water and pushed away from the shore, heading out towards the open water.

"Here I come, Serafina," he said as he paddled away from the remote island that had been his home for the last eight months.

* * *

The water was calm the first couple miles out. When their island home was nearly out of sight, Mario pulled a compass out of his pocket. He had found the old compass on the island about a month earlier.

"We need to sail north," he yelled out to Giuseppe, who was resting for a minute on the opposite end of the boat floor.

"Okay," Giuseppe replied as he once again clutched his chest. Mario knew something was wrong with Giuseppe, but he also knew continuing on was their best chance at survival. They took a small break from paddling and let the boat sail north for a short while.

* * *

When they had been sailing for hours, Mario called out, "Rough seas ahead." Giuseppe grabbed his paddle and rowed hard through the rough tide, as the sea tossed the small boat around like a toy.

Giuseppe had that dull ache in his chest once again, and it was becoming even more persistent. He didn't know how much longer he could go on rowing. He was dehydrated and tired, and he knew the continuing chest pain was not something to ignore.

"I need to lay down," he said to Mario as he stood up and immediately collapsed onto the boat's floor.

"Stay with me, Giuseppe. Rest a while," Mario said. "I will paddle for both of us," he said, taking Giuseppe's oar.

Giuseppe started drifting in and out of consciousness, and as he did so, he had flashbacks of Serafina—memories of the day they met on Via del

Gelso, the amazing night at the Waldorf, and the horrible fight that ended them. He fought to stay awake, to continue on … for Serafina.

CHAPTER 11

~ *Darkness Prevails* ~

SERAFINA WENT ON WITH LIFE THE BEST SHE COULD, MOVING through her days on autopilot as the weeks passed by. She stayed busy at the flower shop, and she started attending church on Sundays with Miss Antoinette and Vincenzo. As she sat in church, she begged God to please bring Giuseppe back home to her somehow.

Following Miss Antoinette's prompting to keep busy, Serafina attended a lot of church functions and made a couple new friends. Miss Antoinette also tried to set her up with a couple nice gentlemen from church, but Serafina had no interest in them. They were nice to talk with, but despite the interest they showed in the beautiful Serafina and the compliments they showered on her, none of them were her Giuseppe.

Serafina spent her evenings in the flower shop, staying for hours after Miss Antoinette went home each day. She took a bottle of wine with her each day, and each evening after her work at the shop was finished, she pulled the wine and her notebook out of her satchel and sat down to write.

My Beloved,

> *The sleepless nights and the melancholy I feel in the wake of your absence hold my heart prisoner—a prisoner to the shattered dreams of our future. The days pass by ever so slowly, some days bearable and some not so much. I keep praying and hoping that you will somehow make it back home to me. I will never be the same me that I was before you sailed out to sea and away from me. I try to hold on and stay positive. I know you are a fighter, my love. I am wearing your ring still, my darling. I wait for you every night and hold out my lantern in hopes that you will see its light and follow it back home to me. I love you forever, my heart.*

> > *Love always,*
> > *Serafina*

Each night after she finished writing a letter to Giuseppe, she finished her wine, tore the letter from her notebook, shoved it into the glass bottle, and corked it shut. She walked down to the jetty and tossed the bottle into the ocean as she held up her lantern, letting it shine out to sea.

The people in town had all started to notice Serafina's strange routine. One night, Miss Antoinette and Vincenzo decided to follow her to the coastline. They watched as she tossed the bottle into the sea and lifted her lantern out over the jetty.

They knew of her heartbreak, and they, too, were distraught over the loss of their good friend, Giuseppe, but they were beginning to worry about her. They tried to involve Serafina in as many outings as they could to try and keep her mind off of his absence. Sometimes she would accept, and other times she couldn't bear to pretend everything was okay with her. On those occasions, she would hide away and break down sobbing, as the pain of losing Giuseppe was just too much to bear.

The fishermen on the docks also knew of Serafina's secret trips out to the jetty. She put on a brave face during the daytime hours, but they all knew of her tremendous heartache and longing for her lover who was lost at sea. They would stand on the docks some nights when they had late boats come in and watch Serafina climb up the jetty and toss her pleas out to the unforgiving tide, as she held up her lantern in hopes that the light would guide Giuseppe home.

Serafina and Miss Antoinette had a large job coming up for the Waldorf Christmas Gala. They had been working endlessly on the beautiful arrangements. Serafina noticed she often didn't feel well lately and thought she might be coming down with the flu.

Miss Antoinette also noticed Serafina wasn't feeling well. "You should go home and rest," Miss Antoinette told her.

"I'm okay," Serafina insisted as she continued working.

"Okay, well let me know if you need a break," Miss Antoinette said in a concerned voice, worried that Serafina's drive to keep herself busy was exhausting her and beginning to impact her health.

* * *

As the days passed, Serafina felt more and more tired. Her appetite gradually decreased until it was almost non-existent, and Miss Antoinette watched as she grew thinner and thinner. Miss Antoinette was worried and finally went over to see Serafina's parents and express her concern. Maybe they knew something that would put her mind at ease about Serafina's health. After visiting with them a few minutes, she learned that they shared her concern, and they all decided it was time to do something.

That night at dinner Serafina's family was gathered around the table. "Serafina, dear, you have barely touched your dinner," her mother said, sounding worried. "I think it is time to go see the doctor. I'm making you an appointment for tomorrow."

After dinner Serafina returned to her bedroom. She grabbed a wine bottle and her sketch of Giuseppe from underneath her bed. She unfolded the sketch onto her bed as she traced her fingers over his sketched face and sobbed. She then pulled her notebook from her satchel and wrote:

My Beloved,

> *My days have been so empty. I can feel you when I close my eyes. You sing me through my darkness. I dance through the pain of your absence. Pain has never felt so real. Losing you is an inconsolable, uncurable, and uncontrollable pain. The pain has turned me into a writer, a poet, and an artist. I try my best to be strong, my love, but the weight hangs heavy on this heart of mine. I always awake in the morning with a new hope that today will be the day you come home to me. I spend my days with a smile on my face and my nights with tears falling from my eyes. Your departure was so sudden. You swore to stay for-ever. My heart has no more words, my soul has lost its song. My heart is empty without you. All that remains inside its chambers is empty red liquid that pumps some semblance of life through the hollow shell of my soul that remains after the wake of your loss hit my life. Blank stares of utter nothingness*

escape my eyes as the tears weep over my soul and well into pools that fall from my dead, lifeless, green eyes that once held love, faith, and happiness. Please my love, look for the light in the night. That is me guiding you back home. I love you forever and always.

Serafina

She tore out the page and rolled it up, sticking it into the bottle and corking it shut as usual. She grabbed her lantern off her nightstand and headed out the door towards the jetty.

A few minutes later, Serafina's father knocked on her door to check on her. "Serafina?" he called out. There was no answer.

"Serafina?" he called again as he slowly opened the bedroom door. The room was empty, and she was gone, along with the lantern. He knew exactly where she was, and it broke his heart. He gently closed her bedroom door.

* * *

Serafina and her mother sat in the small doctor's office in town. Dr. Declamenti was known to be one of the best doctors on the coast.

"Serafina," the nurse called out. "Come on back," she said, smiling. "I'm going to get your height and weight." She gestured for Serafina to step up onto the scale.

"One hundred pounds," the nurse said, causing Serafina's mother to grimace. She realized that Serafina had lost a good thirty pounds over the last month.

The nurse led them back into an exam room with a table covered in paper. "Have a seat. The doctor will be in shortly," she instructed with a smile as she left, closing the door behind her.

Serafina sat up on the large table hanging her feet off the edge, wishing she was with Miss Antoinette at the flower shop, instead of here in this sterile doctor's office. It was only about five minutes before a knock on the door announced the doctor's arrival.

"Hello," Dr. Declamenti said as he walked in. "It seems you haven't been feeling too well, huh?" he asked.

"No, I haven't been feeling myself lately," Serafina told him. "I have been very tired, with an aching feeling throughout my body. I haven't had much of an appetite, either," she told the doctor. "I thought it was the flu, but it doesn't seem to be going away."

"Okay, let's check you out," the doctor said with a worried lock on his face. He placed the blood pressure cuff on her arm and placed his finger on her wrist. He took her temperature and checked her eyes, ears and throat. He palpated her abdomen, then sent her to collect a urine sample.

"Well, your vitals look good, Serafina, but I would also like to run some bloodwork. Something is causing you to feel so poorly. I will have Nora come back in and draw some blood," he said. "It will take a couple days to get the results back, and I will let you know when they come in," the doctor went on to explain to her.

"Okay," Serafina replied, listlessly.

* * *

When Serafina and Colette arrived back home, Serafina was too tired to go back to the flower shop, letting her mother know just how bad she felt, because the flower shop was practically her favorite place to be.

Colette called Miss Antoinette and let her know Serafina was going to be home resting for the day.

"What happened at the doctor?" Miss Antoinette questioned, worried.

"The doctor did some bloodwork, and we are waiting on results," Colette explained. "And after just the doctor's visit, she is too tired to return to work. I hope they can determine what's going on with her, so we can get our old Serafina back."

"Well, I certainly hope she rests up and starts feeling better soon," Miss Antoinette said.

"Thank you, Antoinette. It means the world to me that you are thinking of her. You mean so much to her," Colette said.

Serafina slept all day for two days. She wasn't eating much either. She was taking in liquids, but not nearly enough. She was definitely taking a turn for the worse. Nevertheless, at night she would climb out of bed with her message in a bottle and her lantern and make her way out to the jetty. Her mother and father would hear the door close behind her, knowing where she was headed, and their hearts would sink a bit lower.

Dr. Declamenti called two days later. "I would like to see you back in the office. I have the results to Serafina's bloodwork," he said to Colette over the phone.

"Okay," she replied, feeling dismayed that the doctor wanted them to come in to discuss the bloodwork results. She had a feeling that wasn't a good sign.

The next day Serafina and her mother found themselves sitting back in the same exam room they were in just two days earlier. Time seemed to stand still as they waited for the doctor to come in. Finally, the knock came and the doctor entered the room.

"Hello," Dr. Declamenti said as he took a seat on the small stool on four wheels. *Why did doctors always sit on that kind of chair?* Serafina wondered. He hugged the manila folder containing her results close to his chest.

"Serafina, there is no easy way to say this. You have leukemia," he said.

"It's cancer?" her mother asked, tears filling her eyes.

"Yes, I am afraid so," he said. "I want you to see an oncologist at St. Vincent's in Rome."

Serafina's eyes filled with tears as she processed the news, and her mother hugged her tightly.

"You will need chemotherapy, and we can't treat you here. I think you have a better shot inland where they have all the new advances in cancer treatment," the doctor said. "I will get you all the information with the contact numbers for oncology at St. Vincent's and other things you will need to know," the doctor said to Colette.

"I am so sorry," he said, addressing them both with compassion in his eyes. Colette continued to hug Serafina, as Serafina sobbed into her chest.

* * *

They left the doctors' office in disbelief, carrying all of the paperwork they needed for the hospital in Rome, still trying to process the news they just received.

When they got home, Rocco and Celeste knew something was wrong, but they were stunned when Colette told them the news. The family spent some time hugging one another and crying together, unable to believe how Serafina's life, along with theirs, had suddenly changed. They knew something was wrong with Serafina, but they never suspected it would be cancer.

The day's events took a lot out of Serafina, and she spent most of her time in bed over the next few days, trying to rest up and come to grips with her diagnosis.

Miss Antoinette called the house to find out how the appointment went, since Serafina hadn't returned to work. She cried when Colette told her, "It's cancer … leukemia," as she had grown to love Serafina like a daughter.

* * *

Colette and Rocco decided to pack up the house and leave for Rome as soon as possible, so Serafina could start treatment right away. They were going to stay with a relative who lived outside of Rome while they got Serafina the treatment she needed.

A week later they were already packing the car to head inland. Serafina looked around her room and laid across her bed. She pulled out her notebook and wrote one last letter. She then slipped it into the empty wine bottle she had on her dresser. She looked at the ring on her finger one last time before tossing it into the bottle with the note.

She took her last walk down to the jetty and tossed the bottle out into the cruel water of the sea that was keeping her true love from her. She held up the lantern and shed a few tears, begging Giuseppe to return, telling him she needed him more than ever now.

* * *

The next morning, they all piled into the car that was packed full of their things. "Can you stop by the flower shop so I can say goodbye to Miss Antoinette?" Serafina asked her father.

"Of course," he replied as he pulled out of the driveway.

When Serafina arrived at the flower shop, the door was open, and the lights were on. Serafina walked into the back room.

"Serafina," Miss Antoinette said as she hugged her tightly. It was the first time she had seen Serafina since she got her terrible news. Tears filled Miss Antoinette's eyes at the sight of Serafina's thin frame and pale face. She found herself at a loss for words, not knowing what she could possibly say that would make this moment easier.

"Your mother has my number so she can call me and update me on how you are doing," Miss Antoinette told her, saying something practical to help maintain her composure.

"Can you do me a favor?" Serafina asked.

"Anything, dear," Miss Antoinette replied.

"If Giuseppe comes back home, tell him I waited for him, tell him that every night I sent him messages of love out to sea, and that I love him," she instructed Miss Antoinette.

"No Serafina, you will tell him. You are going to get better and come back home to us," Miss Antoinette said as she hugged her.

"Goodbye Serafina, be strong, and come home soon." Miss Antoinette waved her family off as they pulled away.

The ride to Rome was about three hours inland. Serafina thought of Giuseppe the whole time.

Chapter 12

~ *Goodbye is but only a word* ~

A COUPLE DAYS LATER SERAFINA AND HER PARENTS SAT inside the Cancer Center at St. Vincent's hospital in Rome. They were waiting on the oncologist to give them her treatment plan. Their anxiety was high, and Rocco even shed a couple tears while they waited.

"Serafina Verratti," a nurse called out. They got up and walked over to the nurse as she led them through the door into the back, following closely behind her.

"Here you are," the nurse said, leading them into a large office with a glass window wall behind a wooden desk. The view of the city was phenomenal. If it weren't for the circumstances, Serafina would have been thrilled to see Rome from this breathtaking perspective. She had spent most of her life on the coast and never even traveled to Rome.

"Hello," they heard the doctor say as he walked in from behind them. He walked around the desk and took a seat in front of the large window. "I'm Doctor Moretti," he said, introducing himself to them, and shaking their hands.

"Serafina, I'm sorry to meet you under these circumstances, but you know you have leukemia, and leukemia is a blood cancer." he explained.

"I'll be honest. The particular type you have is not an easy cancer to treat. The chemotherapy will not be easy, but it is our only choice. We will need to give you a strong regimen of chemotherapy twice a week. Meanwhile, we will be looking for a bone marrow donor in order to try and give you the best fighting chance at survival," the doctor said.

"The best fighting chance at survival?" Serafina said. "You mean I may not survive this?"

"We are going to do everything we can to help you fight and survive this disease. We'll admit you this evening and run some more blood work. We will also be swabbing your mouth for DNA to help us find a bone marrow donor that is a match for you.

"Finding a donor is not always easy, but hopefully we can find one in time. I know this is all very hard for you to hear, but I have to make you aware of your current situation," he said, looking at their family with a sorrowful face.

Serafina's mother and father dabbed at their eyes, fighting their tears as they tried to stay strong for Serafina, in light of the news they had just received.

"Can we stay here at the hospital with her as she receives treatment?" Colette asked.

"Of course," the doctor said. "You can stay with her during the day, and if she needs to stay overnight, all the rooms are equipped with pull out sleepers. There is a large cafeteria downstairs and a chapel as well," the doctor replied.

"I just have to ask you a couple questions before we get you admitted, Serafina. They are uncomfortable questions, but we have to ask them. Do you have a living will?" he asked.

"No", Serafina replied. "Who has a living will, or any kind of will at my age?"

"Are you an organ donor?" he asked. She looked over at her mother who was sobbing into her father's chest as the doctor asked his questions that emphasized the seriousness of Serafina's diagnosis.

"Yes, I've always wanted to be an organ donor, but I've never completed the paperwork," she answered.

"Ok, Serafina," he replied. "Are you willing to donate organs if your death is imminent?" he asked. "I know these are hard questions, but we need the answers on record," the doctor said to them with empathy.

"Yes," she answered.

"Do you give your consent?" he addressed Rocco and Colette, acknowledging she was too young to make this decision without her parents' approval. They nodded, solemnly.

"Okay, I need you to sign here," the doctor said as he pushed the paper in front of Serafina and handed her his pen. She grabbed the pen and quickly signed on the dotted line he specified on the paper, before he handed the document to her parents and had them do the same.

* * *

That night Serafina was admitted to the ninth-floor oncology unit. She had a large, private room with a window overlooking the city. There was a large pull out couch under the window. She walked around the room getting accustomed to what would be her main living space for an undetermined amount of time.

An hour later a nurse arrived, introducing herself as Luisa, and placed Serafina's IV and took her vitals. She was a slightly heavy, motherly woman, and Serafina instantly liked her. She returned a few minutes later with Serafina's first dose of chemotherapy and explained to her all about how the chemotherapy worked and some things she may experience while on it, helping put Serafina's mind at ease with her thorough explanations and warm smile.

The nurse hooked her line up to the clear bag with a large red warning label on it that read, "Toxic Chemotherapy." Serafina looked up at it and for a moment couldn't believe what was happening. This had all happened so fast.

* * *

Several hours later Serafina was in the small bathroom in her room feeling miserable. She was sweating, having chills and shakes. She was nauseous and dry heaving into the porcelain toilet, and she sobbed at her condition as she leaned over the toilet. Her mother had come into the bathroom and was sitting behind her on the cold tile floor, rubbing her back as tears streamed down her face, too.

"You can do this," Colette encouraged her, not knowing what else to say. It broke her heart to see Serafina undergoing such an ordeal.

The following morning, Serafina was tired from being up sick most of the night. The nurse gave her some anti-nausea medication and a sleeping pill. She was pretty weak and fatigued the whole morning and desperately needed the rest the medication provided.

Miss Antoinette called Colette at the hospital to check up on Serafina and find out how her first treatment had gone. Colette cried as she told her all about the dreadful night.

Miss Antoinette was devasted by the news. She offered some words of encouragement, as she hoped and prayed for Serafina to get better soon.

* * *

Serafina spent the next couple of days receiving more chemotherapy, while spending her nights fighting the war raging within her body. Terribly nauseous, she couldn't keep any food or liquids down, and the nurses were running fluids through her IV to keep her hydrated. She was down to almost ninety pounds. Her hair started falling out in clumps, and she was already nearly bald.

Celeste went downstairs to the hospital gift shop and bought Serafina a pretty, pink cap. When she returned, she lovingly placed it on Serafina's head.

"It looks beautiful," Celeste said smiling, trying to cheer Serafina up, and the truth was that even in her frail condition, Serafina was still quite lovely. Celeste held her hand while she lay almost lifeless in her hospital bed, thinking about what her sister had gone through within the past few months—falling in love, getting engaged, breaking up, losing her love at sea, and now this—leukemia. Sitting there with her sister, Celeste wished she had been more supportive and spent more time with her.

The doctor came in to talk with Serafina and her family about her blood count numbers and the status of her bone marrow donor. The news was not what they had expected or hoped for.

Serafina's body was resisting the chemotherapy, and her cancer cells were increasing. They were still working on a marrow donor, but had not yet been able to find even a preliminary match to her rare AB Positive blood type.

"I know Serafina is quite ill from the chemo, but unfortunately, we need to be a bit more rigorous," the doctor said. "I am going to try a different chemo drug, and we are broadening our search for a marrow donor, as well," he said, giving them hope to continue to fight.

* * *

A couple more days passed. Serafina was even sicker on the new chemo drugs, and her condition continued to worsen. Her delicate body was even thinner, and she no longer had the strength to get out of bed. The nurse called the doctor to alert him of her rapidly declining condition. It was around lunchtime when the doctor came in to check on Serafina.

After examining Serafina and reviewing her chart, the doctor asked if he could talk to Colette and Rocco in the hallway. Serafina watched them through the door from her bed, knowing the news was not good, but almost too weak to care.

"Her condition is not good," the doctor said. "The cancer is continuing to advance, and her body is not responding to the treatment. We have done everything we can. Her organs will start to shut down soon," the doctor said placing a hand on Colette's shoulder. "I'm sorry I don't have better news, but I think you need to begin making final arrangements for Serafina and prepare to say your goodbyes."

Rocco and Colette broke down crying. Serafina watched from the bed and shed a tear, knowing that the doctor had just given her parents the bad news she already knew in her heart. She knew her time was running out. She could feel it. She didn't need any report to tell her that.

"I think it would be best if we help her a bit by putting her on life support when the time comes. It will help her breathe a little better and make her more comfortable, and it will also preserve her organs since she is a donor," the doctor said, looking at them. It was never easy breaking the news to distraught parents that their child isn't going to make it.

"Serafina could save a life, or maybe even a few lives," the doctor said with a soft smile, attempting to offer them something positive out of the worst news they had ever received.

Rocco nodded his head in agreement, as Colette sobbed uncontrollably into his chest.

"We will wait until she falls into a comatose state, and then we will put her on the ventilator," the doctor advised them. "It will be the best way. I recommend you spend as much time with her as you can while she is awake, and tell friends and family to come visit and say their goodbyes," he said.

Colette made calls to Nonna and other family members, letting them know Serafina's condition was terminal and recommending they come and see her. The last, and most difficult call she made was to Miss Antoinette. She knew how close the two were.

"She isn't doing well," Colette said to Miss Antoinette, trying not to cry. "The doctors advised us to have friends and family come and say their goodbyes." Miss Antoinette sobbed into the phone.

"I just can't believe this is happening. It is so sudden. Vincenzo and I will be there as soon as we can, though," Miss Antoinette told Colette.

* * *

"I can't believe this is happening. First Giuseppe, and now Serafina!" Miss Antoinette said to Vincenzo as they packed the car up, getting ready to head into Rome.

"Never did I expect to have to say goodbye to Serafina. She's too young. She has her whole life ahead of her," Miss Antoinette sobbed. Vincenzo came around to the back hatch of the car where Antoinette was loading the last suitcase in and folded her in his warm embrace as she sobbed.

* * *

Back at the hospital, family members came to visit Serafina. She told them all about Giuseppe and their amazing night at the Waldorf.

"I had the love of my life," she told them. "Do not be sad for me. I will soon be with my love again," she said with a smile to Nonna. "I lived a real-life fairytale."

Serafina's father, mother, and Celeste spent all their time by her bedside. They were saddened, yet comforted, at how accepting Serafina was of her terminal illness. The family laughed and relived old memories during those final days.

CHAPTER 13
~ *No place like Home* ~

BACK IN MIDORI IT WAS A BEAUTIFUL, SUNNY, CLEAR FRIDAY
in February. The fishermen on the dock were busy getting ready to unload
the boats that were due to come in around 11:00 a.m. One of the fishermen
on the dock was getting the nets ready, as he caught a glimpse of what
looked like a large piece of driftwood floating in the sea. It appeared to be
about a mile or so offshore.

"Jake, come and look at this," the fisherman called out. Jake left the
fishery and walked over to the end of the dock next to the fisherman.

"What *is* that?" Jake asked. "Looks like a large piece of driftwood."

"Large?" The fisherman said. "It must be gigantic, especially it we're
able to spot it from this far out," he said in surprise.

* * *

Mario had been paddling for days. He was tired, and his arms felt like jelly. He knew he couldn't continue on like this much longer, and Giuseppe's condition had continued to worsen.

Mario lifted up his head, and as he did, he caught his breath. He could see lights far off in the distance, and he thought he heard muffled voices, too.

"Oh, my God!" he yelled. "Giuseppe! Giuseppe! Look! The coast!"

Giuseppe moaned as his body laid nearly lifeless on the wooden floor of the boat. He was coming in and out of consciousness. Mario tore a piece of Giuseppe's red shirt and tied it to one of the oars as he raised it in the air.

"Help! Help!" he yelled as he waved the oar frantically in the air, hoping to catch someone's attention.

* * *

"Do you hear that? Listen," Jake said. The fishermen were silent for a moment, and in the distance, they heard a very faint cry.

"What is that?" Ben asked Jake as he came over. "It looks like a red glimmer over by that large piece of driftwood out there."

"Hel-l-lp! Hel-l-lp!" Mario yelled as he paddled in closer with the remaining oar.

"There is someone out there," Ben said. "Go get me the binoculars from inside the fishery—quick!" Jake said to Ben. Ben ran off and returned just as quickly, handing over the pair of binoculars to Jake.

"Holy shit," he cried out. "Holy shit! It's Mario! Quick, get to the small motorboat and start the engine!" Jake ordered Ben. They ran over to the boat and hopped in. Jake untied the boat from the dock and sped out towards the approaching craft.

"Look, Giuseppe! We are home! WE ARE HOME!" Mario yelled in excitement as he saw the motorboat approaching.

"Ughhh," was all Giuseppe was able to moan from where he lay on the floor of the boat.

The motorboat was getting closer and closer. "Mario!" Ben cried out as the men approached the makeshift boat, as he wasn't yet able to see Giuseppe in the boat as well. "It's a miracle. It's a miracle!" Ben yelled. It had been almost a full eight months since the storm. Jake pulled the motorboat up close to the tattered wooden boat, and Ben began helping Mario into the boat.

"It's Giuseppe," Mario said. "He is not well." Jake and Ben looked over, surprised to see Giuseppe lying in the homemade boat. The fishermen quickly helped him up and pulled him into the motorboat, then hastily cranked the motor and sped inland.

"When we get to the dock, I want you to immediately run into the fishery and call an ambulance," Jake instructed Ben. "I will stay with Giuseppe until they arrive." Ben nodded. They both knew they didn't have much time if Giuseppe was going to make it.

The fishermen up on the docks saw the boat fast approaching. They all waited in a large crowd for the boat to near the dock, eager to learn how Mario had managed to survive and make it back.

When the motorboat reached the dock, Ben quickly tied the boat securely and ran to the fishery as fast as he could. The men swarmed to the boat, shocked to see both Mario and Giuseppe, and helped Jake unload Giuseppe's limp body onto the dock. Someone ran into the fishery and retrieved a warm jacket for Mario. Others grabbed blankets from the back room in the fishery where the bunks were and ran out to Jake, who had Giuseppe lying on his back on the dock. They covered him with warm blankets.

Soon they heard sirens blaring in the distance and the fisherman could hear them getting louder and louder as they approached the dock. The people in town also heard the sirens and started coming out of their homes and shops to see what was going on at the dock.

It was only about a matter of minutes until the emergency teams showed up. "Back up," they yelled to the fishermen huddling around Giuseppe and Mario.

"We need a chopper," one of the medics called out to another. The medic hit the button on the walkie talkie that hung from his shirt.

"Control, over," a woman's voice came over the radio.

"I need a chopper at the docks off Via del Gelso in Midori—stat, over," the medic responded.

Copy that, chopper to the docks off Via del Gelso in Midori, over," the woman's voice called out once more from the walkie.

The chopper arrived within minutes and hovered over the dock. "Clear the area," the medics yelled to the fishermen on the deck.

"Give the chopper room to land!" another medic called out.

The men distanced themselves, ducking against the strong wind from the chopper's blades, as the helicopter slowly hovered over the dock and touched down. The medics jumped out and pulled an orange backboard out of the helicopter. They called five fishermen back over and had the men pick up Giuseppe all together while they slid the backboard underneath him.

The flight nurse jumped out of the chopper's side door and opened a hatch in the back, and the medics loaded the backboard into the hatch onto a bed that was secured inside. The flight nurse hopped in and started to tie Giuseppe down.

"He needs a trauma unit," one of the medics yelled to the nurse so she could hear him over the noise from the chopper's blades.

"We will be there in less than ten minutes," the nurse responded as she slammed the back hatch closed. The medic tapped the side of the chopper, letting the pilot know it was time to take off. The chopper's blades spun faster, and it lifted off the dock, rose into the air and headed off.

"Mario, Mario," a woman's voice called out. A short, dark-haired, very pregnant woman ran across the deck towards the fishery.

"Maria?" Mario cried out as he heard her voice calling for him.

Maria ran through the door to the fishery. Mario stood up, and she nearly tackled him in a huge hug.

"I thought you were dead. Gone forever!" she said sobbing.

"No, my love," he said. "You kept me alive … you and our baby," he said, touching her large, very pregnant belly.

The medics escorted Mario and Maria to the ambulance out front so Mario could get checked out at the hospital, while the chopper carrying Giuseppe headed toward the nearest trauma center. It was due to land in eight minutes on the rooftop helipad at St. Vincent's Hospital in Rome. Doctors and nurses were alerted by the flight medics and were outside on the rooftop waiting for Giuseppe as the chopper approached.

CHAPTER 14

~Heart to Heart~

IT WAS FRIDAY MORNING. SERAFINA HAD SLIPPED INTO A coma the night before, and her doctors and nurses had placed her on the respirator to keep her comfortable and give her loved ones time to say goodbye before the doctor removed her from the life support and kept her comfortable as they let her slowly leave them.

Celeste spent the night holding her sister's hand and crying. Their mother and father slept on and off, taking turns by Serafina's bedside as well.

Antoinette and Vincenzo arrived shortly after the nurse made her morning rounds. They hugged Rocco and Colette and cried with them.

Miss Antoinette sat by Serafina's bed, holding her hand as she told her about all that was going on back in Midori with the flower shop and church. She cried as she told Serafina how she was going to make the most beautiful flower arrangements for her funeral.

"Serafina, beautiful Serafina," Vincenzo said as he took her hand. "You always dreamed of love and beauty. I am so happy you and Giuseppe found that in one another. You radiated love, Serafina.

"You brought Antoinette and I together and made us so happy," he said, looking at Antoinette. "Now it is time for you to be with Giuseppe again," he said as he cried.

"Trauma Team One, Trauma Team One," they all heard, as it came blasting over the speakers of the hospital.

"I hate hospitals," Colette said. "I hate that Serafina can't have quiet right now." From Serafina's room they could hear the sound of the helicopter hovering over the hospital.

"What is going on?" Miss Antoinette asked the nurse who came in to check on Serafina.

"We have a trauma coming in on the rooftop," the nurse told them.

"How sad," Celeste said, as she sat beside Serafina, still holding her sister's hand.

* * *

The chopper landed on the helipad and the flight nurse opened the hatch. The trauma team rushed over to the hatch and pulled out the stretcher. They rushed Giuseppe quickly into the hospital and directly to the intensive care unit.

Doctors and nurses surrounded Giuseppe, taking his vitals and delivering medications and fluids through his IV. The cardiologist entered the room and examined him, his face betraying his concern as he proceeded.

"I need an ultrasound machine—stat," the doctor said. Moments later, a nurse wheeled in an ultrasound machine, and the doctor placed the wand over Giuseppe's heart.

"He has a myocardial rupture, and his heart is severely damaged," the doctor called out. Without a new heart he won't survive very long. We need to call the Transplant Centre and get him on the transplant list as soon as possible," the doctor said to the ICU nurse.

The nurse rushed over to the phone and dialed the National Italian Transplant Centre. After being placed on hold for what seemed like forever, her call was finally answered.

Yes, this is Natalia Russo. I am a nurse at St. Vincent ICU. I need to put a patient on the urgent procurement list for a heart," she told the woman on the other end of the line.

"What is his blood type?" the woman on the phone asked.

The nurse looked at Giuseppe's chart and answered, "Yes, his blood type is AB positive," she told the woman, feeling her heart sink.

"That is a very rare blood type," the woman from the transplant center said, confirming what the ICU nurse already knew. "It may be difficult to procure a donor heart that is a match," she told Natalia grimly. "Let me search the database. Please hold."

"Natalia?" the woman said, returning to the conversation.

"Yes?" Natalia answered.

"We don't have a donor heart available that matches your patient," the woman said. "But do you know there is a donor right in your hospital whose blood type is AB positive? The patient is terminally ill and is currently on life support. The patient is also registered as an organ donor," the woman told her.

"Really?" the nurse said, incredulous. She knew the odds of this happening were unbelievably low.

"Yes, and the transplant surgical team is already standing by downstairs. We would just need to confirm that the recipient meets the criteria for the heart and get the proper authorization.

"The donor patient's name is Serafina Verratti. She is on the ninth floor in Oncology," the woman said.

"Thank you so much. Please let me know when you receive the authorization," Natalia said. She hung up the phone and immediately called the ninth floor.

"Hello, Oncology," the nurse answered.

"Hello, this is Natalia from the trauma ICU upstairs. Do you have a patient by the name of Serafina Verratti?" she asked the nurse.

"Yes," the nurse replied.

"Who is her oncologist?" Natalia asked.

"Dr. Labonne," the nurse responded.

"May I speak with him? It's urgent," Natalia asked.

"Sure, let me see if he is on the floor, Natalia." the nurse said as she put her on hold.

* * *

Dr. Labonne was in Serafina's room, speaking to Rocco and Colette. "Doctor, I'm sorry to interrupt, but I have the Trauma ICU on the phone. They need to speak with you," the nurse told him.

"If you will excuse me for a second," the doctor said to Serafina's mother and father and quickly disappeared from the room.

Fifteen minutes later, Dr. Labonne returned to Serafina's room. "I need to speak with you both," he said, looking at Rocco and Colette, solemnly.

"As we've already discussed, we've done everything for Serafina that we can. She doesn't have very much time left, but her organs are still viable," he said looking at them.

"We have a trauma patient upstairs who needs a heart transplant to survive, and your Serafina is his perfect match. It is your decision to make whether or not you want to take her off the machines and specify our patient to be the recipient of Serafina's heart when she passes, but I urge you to please think about it and consider it carefully.

Our patient needing the heart transplant is a twenty-two-year-old young man, and he can continue to live with Serafina's gift of a heart. If Serafina donates her heart to him, she will not die in vain. She will die having saved a life," the doctor told them."

Rocco's eyes met Colette's. Celeste looked at Miss Antoinette and Vincenzo who sat beside Serafina, holding her other hand.

"Will you give us permission to use her heart for donation to our patient who needs it?" the doctor asked.

Rocco looked at Colette, then back at the doctor with tears in his eyes, as he nodded his head, yes.

"Thank you so much," Dr. Labonne said. He walked over to Serafina's bedside.

"Thank you, Serafina. Your heart shall go on beating," he said.

They all cried as Dr. Labonne removed the tube from Serafina's throat. "Now we just keep her comfortable and wait. It should not be very long until she is gone," he said.

Less than an hour later, Serafina peacefully passed away, surrounded by her family and her dearest friends. They bid her their final goodbyes, and then Dr. Labonne returned with the transplant surgical team. Rocco, Colette, Celeste, Miss Antoinette, and Vincenzo all cried as they kissed her goodbye, one-by-one. The transplant team quickly unsnapped the locks from Serafina's bed, then surrounded the rails of her bed as they wheeled her off out of the room.

* * *

"ICU, this is Natalia," the nurse said as she answered the phone.

"Natalia, this is Dr. Labonne. Tell Dr. Serafini to prep his patient. We have his heart."

"Yes, doctor," Natalia said as she shed a tear at the miracle she was witnessing … two patients with rare blood types a match for a heart transplant at the same hospital at the perfect moment.

* * *

Dr. Serafini was listening to Giuseppe's heart once again when Natalia ran into the room.

"Dr. Serafini? Dr. Labonne said to prep the patient. We have a heart!" she cried out. The trauma team cheered.

"Well, isn't this a beautiful day," Dr. Serafini said. "Giuseppe, you have an angel watching over you," he said to Giuseppe's unconscious body.

"Yes," Natalia said with tears in her eyes. "Her name is Serafina!"

* * *

It had been a week since the transplant, and Giuseppe was recovering beautifully. Dr. Serafini told him that not many patients adjust to a new heart quite as well. They usually struggle with some rejection symptoms while adjusting, but it seemed that this heart was his perfect match.

Giuseppe smiled happily, thinking of how he had a fresh start at life now. He just wanted to get home and see Serafina. He tried calling the flower shop and her father's store several times, but there had been no answer, which he had found strange.

While Giuseppe was in the hospital, his grandparents stayed at a local hotel, traveling back and forth to see him.

"We were so worried," his grandmother said, hugging him.

"I kept your mother and father updated constantly," she assured him.

"The doctor said you can come home tomorrow," Giuseppe's grandfather said, happily.

"Great!" Giuseppe said. "I can't wait to get back!" he said with delight, thinking of just how tightly he was going to hold Serafina when he saw her again.

The next day came quickly, and Giuseppe happily held his discharge papers in his hand. The nurses all came in to say goodbye to him and give him their best wishes. He had charmed them all during his stay, and they were all quite fond of the handsome young fisherman with a new heart.

"You ready, son?" his grandfather asked.

"I couldn't be more ready," Giuseppe replied with a huge smile across his face.

A nurse appeared with a wheelchair. "Your chariot awaits," she said as Giuseppe sat down in it. Everyone in the ICU cheered as they wheeled him to the elevator to begin his journey home.

CHAPTER 15

~The Gift~

GIUSEPPE AND HIS GRANDPARENTS ARRIVED IN MIDORI AT noon. The sun was out, and the sky was a beautiful baby blue with puffy white clouds hanging low. The weather was perfect, and Giuseppe felt like the town was welcoming him home.

His grandparents dropped him off at the dock, as he had requested. He slowly climbed the staircase and walked up onto the deck, careful not to overdo it since he hadn't fully recovered from his surgery and his ordeal at sea.

"Hey look, it's Giuseppe," he heard Ben call out to the men, and cheers broke out. The men hugged Giuseppe and patted him on the back, grateful to have him back, safe and sound.

"Where is Mario?" Giuseppe asked Jake.

"His baby was born last night," Jake said with a grin. "It's a girl!"

Giuseppe smiled, tears of happiness filling his eyes as he heard the good news. "I'll be back," he said. He walked across the deck and back down the stairs to the old familiar cobblestone walk, as he headed towards the flower shop. He took a deep breath in as he quickly straightened his clothes with his hand and fixed his hair.

The lights were on in the flower shop. Giuseppe approached the door and walked in but saw nobody inside.

"I'll be with you in a minute," he heard Miss Antoinette call out. She was looking for something down under the counter when she heard the bells on the door chime.

"Okay, ma'am," she heard a familiar voice call out. She slowly stood up.

"Giuseppe?" she said in disbelief. "Oh my God, Giuseppe!" she cried. She came out from behind the counter and hugged him as she cried tears of joy.

"Where's Serafina?" he asked excitedly, as he looked over into the back room. Miss Antoinette's face fell as she looked at him.

"Serafina got sick," she said.

"Did she go home?" he asked, confused.

"The cancer took her about two weeks ago," Miss Antoinette said with tears in her eyes.

"No!" he cried. "What? No!" he cried in pain, a reminder that his heart was still healing.

"I should have never left her. This is all my fault," he said, crying, running his hands through his hair in anguish.

"No," Miss Antoinette said gently as she hugged him.

"Serafina got sick. There was nothing any of us could do," she said. "She wore your ring every day. She wrote you letters and sent them out to you off the jetty every night for nearly eight months. It killed her to lose you, Giuseppe. She loved you so very much," Miss Antoinette went on to tell him.

"Did she die in pain?" he asked, feeling guilty for not being there for her in her final moments.

"No. We were all at St. Vincent's in Rome the day she passed. Serafina died selflessly. She gifted her heart to a young man who was dying," Miss Antoinette went on telling him.

"St. Vincent's in Rome?" he questioned.

"Yes," Miss Antoinette answered.

"What was the date of her passing?" he asked.

"February tenth," Miss Antoinette answered.

Giuseppe's eyes filled with tears and a large smile came over his face. Miss Antoinette looked at him in confusion. He unbuttoned his plaid shirt to reveal a large scar down his bare chest!

"It was me!" he smiled through the tears. "She saved me," he said. Miss Antoinette stared in utter surprise as tears filled her eyes.

"Can I?" she asked, reaching her hand out toward his scar.

"Go ahead," he said.

Miss Antoinette laid her hand on the long scar down his chest. She put her ear against his chest and sobbed. She could hear the tender thumps of Serafina's heart beating in the chest of the man she loved. She not only became his heart, but she also made it back home.

Miss Antoinette and Giuseppe hugged and cried together for a while in their shared grief and happiness. It was good for both of their hearts to have a good cry together, but they knew there was somewhere else they needed to go.

Miss Antoinette closed up the shop early, and she and Giuseppe headed over to Serafina's family's apartment. They cried in happiness to see him.

Giuseppe told them all about the shipwreck and how he and Mario built the boat to sail back home. He told them he should have died on that island, but Serafina gave him the drive to make it back home. He showed them the scar on his chest and allowed them all to listen to Serafina's heart beating inside it.

Serafina's family told Giuseppe about all her trips out to the jetty and about her lantern. Her father went into her bedroom and grabbed the lantern off the nightstand.

"Here, Giuseppe, I want you to have this, and I know it's what Serafina would have wanted," her father said as he handed him the lantern.

Chapter 16

~*Message in a Bottle*~

IT WAS APRIL IN MIDORI. ROCCO AND COLETTE HAD PLANNED a memorial ceremony for Serafina, and the whole town was invited. Serafina had been cremated, and her parents were saving her ashes for this occasion. They knew if there was one place Serafina would want as her final resting place, it would be at sea with Giuseppe.

Rocco and Giuseppe had been working for weeks, making a large wooden lantern they would place on the dock in her memory. A light inside the lantern would shine brightly over the dock, bright enough to be seen for miles off the coast.

They worked tirelessly night after night, carving out the wood and assembling what they called "Serafina's Lantern." A carving on the outside of the lantern read, "Follow the light. It shall guide you home."

The night before the memorial Giuseppe and Rocco lugged the large lantern to the dock and bolted it down to the wooden deck. It was for sure a sight to behold, Giuseppe thought, but then again, so was Serafina.

"Giuseppe, I want you to have some of Serafina's ashes," Rocco said as he handed him a tiny satchel. Giuseppe took the satchel from his hands and held it close to his chest, treasuring the memory of her, as her heart beat within him.

"You can keep them or spread them however you wish," Serafina's father said. He gave Giuseppe a warm smile, but his eyes were filled with tears.

"Thank you," Giuseppe said, putting his arm around Rocco and pulling him in for a hug, as they took a moment to mourn together for the girl they both loved.

* * *

The next day the dock was packed with people milling about. It was a beautiful day, and the air was full of the sound of children's laughter as the children ran around playing. Everyone took the time to walk around and admire the large lantern, admiring it and sharing gossip among those who had seen Serafina making her trips to the jetty with her small lantern.

People shared stories of Serafina and laughed and cried. Celeste gave a speech about her sister that brought everyone to tears. Nonna talked about how Serafina would come to the vineyard and stomp grapes every summer. Rocco shared stories and made a speech about his beautiful daughter, but Colette couldn't bring herself to make a speech.

Giuseppe got up to the podium and told their love story from beginning to the very end. He opened his shirt and showed them all his scar on his chest, and as he shared that her beating heart was the only reason he was still alive, the entire crowd was in tears. There was not a dry eye on the dock, even among the rugged fishermen.

Finally, it was time to release Serafina's ashes. Miss Antoinette and Vincenzo joined the family as they tossed her ashes over the dock, into the water, bidding her farewell, and wishing her to rest in peace, as they treasured their memories of the special girl who would be deeply missed.

* * *

Giuseppe was cleaning up as everyone was leaving the dock. It felt good to stay busy as his emotions swirled.

"Giuseppe," he heard Mario say from behind him. Giuseppe turned around. Mario was standing next to a short, dark-haired woman who was holding a baby carrier.

"Mario," he said, as he smiled and hugged the man with whom he shared a special bond.

"This is Maria," Mario said, introducing him to the woman.

"Hello, Maria," Giuseppe said smiling.

"And this," Mario said as he bent down and grabbed the tiny baby girl from the carrier, "this is Serafina," Mario said with a large smile.

Giuseppe's eyes filled with tears. He pulled his face in close to the little baby girl.

"Hello, Serafina," Giuseppe said sweetly, with a smile full of wonder and happiness, the new life bringing him a moment of comfort in his sorrow.

* * *

A month passed by, and the weather one particular day was warm and sunny. Beautiful days like this made Giuseppe miss Serafina more than usual.

He looked out at the ocean and thought about her. He pulled out the satchel of her ashes that he usually carried with him. He still had no idea what he wanted to do with them. Keeping them seemed kind of silly, as he had her heart beating inside his chest, living within him.

He walked down Via del Gelso and out to the jetty that she visited with her lantern nightly in his absence according to the stories, holding her lantern up across the sea, calling him home.

Giuseppe climbed up on the slippery, wet, black rocks that Serafina traversed each evening. He took a seat, looking out at the ocean as he held the satchel in his hands. He lifted the satchel and threw it, along with its precious contents, into the water below. He remained there for a time, watching as the bag floated slowly out to sea.

Suddenly, a glimmer from the rocks below caught his eye. *What was that?* He wondered.

Giuseppe climbed down among the rocks, carefully stepping across the slippery stones until he got to the area where he spotted the shimmering item from above. He looked down and finally spotted a tiny glimmer between some of the black rocks. He bent down and removed a couple loose rocks, one-by-one, and the glimmer got brighter. He dug deeper into the rocks of the jetty and discovered what looked to be a small cavern that the tide must have made during the storm. It appeared like the water had a backflow into the cavern.

He stood up and started removing rocks, and what he saw amazed him. Wine bottles! Nearly a hundred of them filled the cavern.

One bottle in particular seemed to be the one that caught his eye from up above. The sun was hitting it just perfectly, and something inside reflected the sunlight more than the others, allowing it to shine up through the rocks.

Giuseppe carefully made his way over to the bottle, and when he picked it up, he discovered there were papers inside. A message in a bottle?

He sat down, uncorked the bottle, and pulled out the papers. He heard a clink in the bottle and cried out in disbelief when he looked inside. Surely, it couldn't be! He tipped the bottle over into his hand and allowed the tiny treasure to slip out. He opened his hand and couldn't believe his eyes. In the palm of his hand sat Serafina's heart-shaped diamond engagement ring. The papers must be messages from her!

Giuseppe opened the first piece of paper. It was a sketch of his face Serafina had drawn with his eyes colored in dark blue. Tears flowed from his blue eyes as he opened the second piece of paper and read the message it contained …

My Beloved Giuseppe,

Every day is Valentine's Day when I am with you! We have a love so beautiful and so true. A love only fairytales are made of. You are every love song that has ever been sung.

I am sick, my love, and it seems my prognosis may not be good. I am praying that whatever happens and wherever we end up in the end, we will be together as one. Our love is timeless. A love not even death can destroy. Keep my heart until we meet again.

Your Forever Valentine,
Serafina

Fine.